THE MOSTLY TRUE TALE OF GETTING ROOFIED IN TOKYO AND WAKING UP MARRIED IN RURAL THAILAND

—— SPECIAL UK EDITION ——

Oscar Slamp

THE MOSTLY TRUE TALE OF GETTING ROOFIED IN TOKYO AND WAKING UP MARRIED IN RURAL THAILAND

SPECIAL UK EDITION

For permission requests, media inquiries, or more information, visit: oscarslamp.com

First Edition Available on Amazon

Special UK Edition: ISBN: 979-8-29-7718777

Editorial Guidance by Suzanne Marie Tienken

Acknowledgments
My thanks to my editor, Suzanne, who helped me sand down the edges without dulling the blade — and to my loving audience in the United Kingdom. This **Special UK Edition** was created in gratitude to the readers of Britain who have embraced Willie and Oscar.

On behalf of Willie, I dedicate this book to Lou.

Table of Contents

Prologue

I met Willie Lyonsan when we were both five years old. My parents bought the house across the street from his in Fitzgerald Acres—a sun-faded subdivision near Beaverton, Michigan, a couple hours south of the Mackinac Bridge. A blink of a town nestled in God's country, where pine forests stretched out like quiet prayers and winters arrived early and stayed long enough to question your resolve. Beaverton was home to maybe 600 souls back then. It hasn't grown much since. It's the kind of place where change goes to die.

Willie's family was... prolific. His grandparents lived between his house and mine, and both of his great-grandmothers—one maternal, one paternal—lived right across the street. Yes, two elderly matriarchs who'd lost their husbands long ago, cohabiting peacefully for fifty years, spending their evenings watching Lawrence Welk and making ice cream floats like they were sacred rites. Willie loved them fiercely. And they him. We'd sit with them most nights, spooning up vanilla ice cream slathered in chocolate syrup, caught in that gentle, sepia-toned routine of an era already beginning to fade. Willie's family lived stitched into the fabric of that little patch of earth.

Willie and I were inseparable back then. We terrorized the neighborhood on anything that had wheels: bikes, snowmobiles, makeshift go-karts, and eventually, motorbikes. If it moved and made noise, it belonged to us. Our orbit was noisy, reckless, and oddly sweet. But when Willie's parents divorced—somewhere around age eight or nine—the atmosphere around him shifted. The safety net was still there, just a little more threadbare.

That said, Willie's family was a study in civility. Salt of the earth, both sides. Even post-divorce, there were no fireworks. No shouting matches or bitter custody disputes. His mom and dad spent holidays together, remarried, and somehow the whole patchwork functioned. Willie's life was reshuffled, yes—but never chaotic.

Even before the divorce, Willie was always testing fences. He had a magnetism wrapped in mischief. If he was told not to do something, he'd do it twice—just to be sure. Not to be difficult. Just to affirm, in his own weird code, that no one got to draw his boundaries for him. Fiercely independent doesn't quite do it justice. He was like a stray dog with a PhD. He was allergic to being told what to do. And yet—there was a kindness under all that bravado. A soft heart that beat hardest for the misfits. A woman who came in and helped with housework once a week predicted to his Mom Willie would become a preacher one day. She was half right.

Throughout school, Willie had a radar for the lonely. The oddballs. The ones who sat alone. He didn't rescue them. He befriended them. Genuinely. And when Willie liked someone, everyone else followed suit. That's how social dynamics worked around him. He was the gravity.

He wasn't a big kid—scrappy, unafraid—but confidence seemed stitched into his DNA. He never had to fight. Wouldn't dream of it. He disarmed with charm. He could talk his way into or out of anything. And people would go to the mat for him, just because. If Willie said hello to the kid who peed his pants sitting alone at lunch, that kid had a lunch table the next day, full of new friends. That was Willie. He redrew social lines with casual ease.

By the time we reached high school, I was equal parts anxious and lost. The building loomed large, intimidating. But Willie? He glided through it like a tour guide. Within weeks, he had us fraternizing with juniors and seniors, trading laughs in places we didn't belong. He broke down the hierarchy by simply ignoring it.

There was a smoking pit behind the school—a small gravel patch just off campus where the tough kids went to pretend they didn't care. Willie fit right in. He'd be out there with a Marlboro and a couple of the special ed kids, laughing like old friends. And somehow, they were. When the new principal, Mr. Pederson, tried to close the pit, everyone talked big. Willie acted. "I'm organizing a walkout," he told us. He was fifteen.

Three days later, he had the school whipped into a frenzy. We staged in the cafeteria, chanting, full of borrowed courage. Willie lit a cigarette in the hall—because of course he did—and shouted, "Pederson sucks!" We marched, like some rebellious parade, past the library, the main office, and right out the front doors to the local convenience store.

His girlfriend's brother tipped off the local newspaper. The news station picked it up. Willie was on TV that night, in the paper the next morning. And the day after? He was in Pederson's office being handed a 33-day in-house suspension. Thirty for the walkout, three for the hallway cigarette. They sent us to the 'Old El' , a half abandoned elementary school—a cold, echoing purgatory where time stood still. It was torture. Like watching paint dry or grass grow. Willie endured it like a Monk. The next day he quit school, with his dad's blessing. Just like that.

He was bored out of his skull. With an IQ hovering near 140, he absorbed information like a sponge but had zero interest in structure. He never studied. Barely showed up. Still carried a C average. He was intuitive, quick, and terrifyingly sharp. But school wasn't built for a mind like his. He needed fire.

And speaking of fire—Willie had a thing for whiskey. Three-quarters Scottish and a quarter German, he inexplicably developed, or maybe inherited a rather sophisticated taste for it early in life. Boilermakers, specifically. Top shelf whiskey with a Hamm's or a PBR back. He loved cheap, Midwest lagers but said cheap liquor made his teeth itch. And while most teenage drinking ended in parking lot fistfights or tearful apologies, Willie's indulgence was celebratory. Joyful. Almost... ceremonial. He didn't drink to forget. He drank to *cheers* the moment.

His penchant for two wheels started early, too. His dad put him into BMX competition at age nine. He was pretty good. Won a few trophies. His mom—perhaps in a devilish way to one-up his old man—got him a mini bike.

That was it. He graduated to full on motocross competition by twelve. He was hooked.

He wasn't reckless, just endlessly kinetic. Speed skating. Hockey. Once we ice skated across a frozen lake to go to the roller rink. We roller skated the night away. Then we ice skated back under the stars.

He lived on the edge of motion. He knew the ER staff by name. Broke every finger, at least once. An arm, an ankle, collarbone. Stitches. Concussions. Dislocated joints. They kept his chart at the front desk. He'd often show up solo, bleeding and apologizing for the inconvenience.

When he was sixteen, he got into a drinking contest with a local rich kid and somehow walked away having traded a car stereo for the kid's Kawasaki KZ900. With witnesses. No one blinked. The next day, they met in the park, shook hands, made the swap. That's how things worked in our town. Words meant something.

He loved that motorcycle. Rain or shine, he rode that bike like it owed him money. One day he picked me up and said, "Let's see how far we can get on a tank of gas." We rode for hours, ended up in Fort Wayne, Indiana. On the way back, we hit a rainstorm of biblical proportion just outside Lansing. "Should we stop under one of these overpasses?" I shouted.

"Nah, we'll be fine," he yelled back, belly laughing like a lunatic.

Rain fell like bullets. I held on for dear life. He howled like a madman. It was freezing. And it was one of the best days of my life. We were nineteen. Not old enough to drink, legally. But after we made it back, soaked, half-blind and exhausted, we found a quiet little late night greasy spoon to grab a bite. We sat at the bar and told the bartender our story. She smiled, brought us burgers and beers, and told us to sit in the back. Different times.

Willie has what I've come to call untamed intelligence. He can do anything. Build a company from scratch. Nail branding, messaging, design. He'll get clients— sometimes huge ones. Then he'll walk away. There's a trail of abandoned brilliance behind him, like half-built cathedrals. It's maddening.

I once asked him why. Over boilermakers. He got quiet. Withdrawn. Sad, even. He mumbled something about timing, or maybe worthiness. Then he re-animated back into good ol' Willie. But I think... I think he doesn't believe he deserves to win.

He once created a consulting firm so convincing that his dad thought he'd bought into a franchise. He landed a 21-plant energy analysis contract across five states by pitching a guy at a networking event—despite having no actual team or relevant experience. He called a retired engineer friend the next day to ask what he'd promised. He pulled it off. Then let it die.

His love life? Predictably dramatic. With the exception of the year or so he spent alone after the Maria incident—that one nearly killed him, but we'll get back to that one later—he was always in the company of beautiful women. And, I think because of his obsession with far away places, they were always... international. "He has a type, doesn't he?" Bruce, our bartender friend, once whispered to me. Korea. Mexico. Africa. India. Then came the Native American medicine woman he somehow wrangled in Arizona. Highly regarded across multiple tribes she had been conducting psilocybin ceremonies under the desert moonlight for 20 years.

Willie wasn't into drugs. We dabbled with weed as kids, but that was it. Still, he agreed, no doubt mostly under the influence of her beauty. Three days of prep—hydration, meditation, no booze. She even created a medicine wheel with stones for him to sit in the middle of for the ceremony. Everything was set. The night was perfect. Full moon. Cool still air. A fire crackling. The desert was aglow. The moment of truth. She gave him chocolate infused with psilocybin.

They waited. Nothing happened. She was baffled. She gave him another dose. Still nothing. Not a flicker of color. Not a hint of sound. He laughed. A mixture of embarrassment and reaction to his laughing, she was not happy.

"The medicine couldn't catch up to me," he told me later.

Needless to say, that relationship didn't last.

And you couldn't really talk about Willie without mentioning Lou—his thick-set Boston Bull and constant companion. They moved through the world like two halves of the same thought. No leash. No collar. Just an unspoken bond, like gravity. Louie had his own bar stools, his own code of conduct, and the kind of presence that turned laminated "No Dogs Allowed" signs into punchlines. Willie rigged a custom seat on his motorcycle for him to ride in— goggles on, scarf flapping, stone-faced up front like a general leading a parade. He never barked, never strayed, and somehow always knew exactly where to be. People liked to say Louie wasn't really a dog at all, just an old jazz man reincarnated—quiet, steady, and a little bit magic.

Willie always had one foot out the door. Beaverton couldn't hold him—it never could. His mind was forever on something bigger, drawn to faraway places like some internal compass that refused to settle. Raised by creatives—

luthiers, writers, artists, musicians—it was only natural he'd find his own voice behind a lens. Cameras became his instrument, film and photography his medium, storytelling his instinct. A natural raconteur, he told stories like breathing—never for profit (he was allergic to profit), but, just because...

He converted to Buddhism, searching, always searching, for something more meaningful. And while he had a grand, adventurous spirit, he also carried a heart bigger than his chest could rightly contain—the kind that bled for others, even when it meant carving pieces off for people who had no intention of giving anything back. There wasn't a damn thing he wouldn't do for someone he loved, even if it broke him. And break him it did. In the handful of years leading up to that fabled pilgrimage to Japan, I watched my old friend hollow out. Slowly. Quietly. Like a house eaten by termites—still standing, but barely. The lights were on, but nobody was home anymore. Not really.

It all started with a girl, of course. Doesn't it always? But this wasn't some passing romance or one-night regret. Willie fell hard—*harder than I've ever seen a man fall*. He gave her everything. And when that wasn't enough, he dug deeper, offering up parts of himself he couldn't afford to lose. She came wrapped in red flags and heartache, dragging a storm behind her, and Willie just stood there in the rain, arms wide open. He didn't flinch. Didn't blink. He *believed*. He believed love could fix it. That *he* could fix it.

But she wasn't looking to be fixed. Not really. And loving her became a kind of slow suicide. One sacrifice at a time, one compromise after another, he dimmed his own light to keep her world from going dark. Until, eventually, he was just a shadow—a ghost of the man I once knew. He stopped laughing. Stopped showing up. Even Louie—you could tell by watching him he didn't fully recognize his old pal anymore.

It all came to a head in the quiet hours—the kind of long, sleepless nights that turn your own thoughts against you. He told me once, not long after, that he'd stood at the edge of the void more than once. Not metaphorically. Not poetically. *Literally.* Stared into it. Felt it tugging at him. The way your feet can't find the bottom of the pool when you've wandered to close to the deep end. He never jumped, but he didn't walk away either. He *lingered*. Teetered. And in some strange, impossible way, it was the pain itself that kept him alive. Like it was proof he still had something left to lose.

He left after that. The last I knew he was bouncing around Southeast Asia. He'd gotten himself into quite a pickle over there. He told me the story, at least what he remembers of it. I know all of Willie's stories and I've never heard one like this. I went to see him. I had to. I had to see it first hand. I heard both sides, although I don't think either of them fully know for sure what happened. It's a hell of a tale though....

Scene 1

The Unraveling

Stumbling recklessly down a narrow, dimly lit alleyway in Tokyo's bustling Ota Ward, not far from Haneda International Airport, Willie's vision swam with blurs and indistinct shapes. Holding his stomach, bent over in agony, his steps were unsteady, weaving a crooked path as if guided by an invisible hand. The neon colors of the night lights were softened and distorted, swirling in chaotic patterns that danced before his eyes, making it a herculean task just to put one foot in front of the other. Pedestrians eyed him with a mix of curiosity and caution, sidestepping to avoid his erratic, zigzagging progress along the sidewalk. In his clouded mind, a single thought emerged with clarity: if he could just find some cold water to pour over his head, he might regain the senses he'd lost.

With this hope, he spotted a 7-11 along his route and tumbled in, nearly falling in the process. The fluorescent lights of the store cast a harsh, sterile glow over his disheveled figure. Barely managing to maintain his balance, he hunched over like a man who had braved a tempest, each movement a betrayal of his intentions, as if the very earth conspired to trip him. He squinted through the haze, trying to fix his gaze on what he hoped was a water cooler. Yet, after only a few faltering steps inside the store, he felt the weight of curious eyes and judgmental stares upon him. He wavered like a spinning top on the verge of collapse, muttering incoherently under his breath before turning and stumbling back out into the night.

Somewhere along the bustling street between the fluorescent glow of the 7-11 and the comfort of his hotel, he reached into his back pocket, pulled out his phone and somehow managed to call his friend and neighbor, Wasum.

Though she was still cocooned in the warmth of morning sleep, the persistent ring of her phone pierced through her dreams. With a groggy sigh, she fumbled around the nightstand, finally grasping the device to see it was Willie calling. She answered.

"Willie. Are you ok?"

She could hear him attempting to speak, with city noises in the background, as he mumbled and fiddled with his phone. She couldn't decipher what he was trying to communicate. However, knowing that Willie was never too far out of control, no matter how intoxicated, Wasum quickly became alert and concentrated on the call.

"Willie. Willie! Are you there?"

She checked the app—they had programmed each other into the Find My app on their phones. She could see he was in Tokyo, a short distance from Haneda airport. She knew he was due to come home from his trip the day before, but hadn't heard from him. She figured he was in the RV sleeping off jet lag and getting reacclimated to mountain time again. She was surprised to see he was still in Japan, which heightened her concern.

"Willie! Willie! Are you there?" The phone went silent.

Wasum's older brother, Decha, who was brought up by their aunt following their father's death, worked as a cargo plane pilot under subcontract with SIAM Shipping and a few other charter companies based in Bangkok. His job involved delivering goods, and occasionally people, across Asia, and he frequently flew into Kansai, Narita, and

Haneda. When she contacted him, it turned out by sheer luck that he was on a layover in Osaka, having just completed a delivery of fresh bananas and dried mangoes to a client at Kansai International Airport.

"Wasum! What's up, Sister?"

"You remember my friend Willie, my neighbor I told you about?"

"Yep."

"I think he's in big trouble in Tokyo…" she explained, telling him about the uncharacteristic phone call. "Do you have any contacts at Haneda who could check on him, or is there any way you can help?"

Decha replied, "Let me see what I can do. I might even be able to get over there. I was deadheading back but trying to find a load or a charter. I'll make some more calls. I'll call you back."

Wasum checked the app again and could see Willie, or at least his phone, was at the Oriental Express Hotel, about 15-20 minutes from the airport. She texted Decha with the location. Feeling helpless, all she could do was wait.

An hour had passed and finally Decha called.

"I found a load out of Haneda with another carrier, and I've got a friend—a local there who's pretty well connected in Tokyo. I scored a standby seat on the next flight over. He's going to meet me there."

"Oh my Buddha! Thank you, Decha."

"I'll call as soon as I know anything." He replied.

Several hours went by, and it was almost 1 PM in Arizona, 5 AM in Tokyo. The app indicated that Willie was still close to or possibly inside the Oriental Express, which Wasum took as a positive sign. She knew that this was the hotel where he planned to spend the last few nights before his scheduled flight home. Just then, her phone rang.

"Decha?"

"We're here at the hotel looking for him, *under the radar*..."

"What do you mean, *under the radar*??"

Decha replied, "Turns out my friend here knows the girl at the front desk of the hotel. She told him the police came in looking for Willie. Apparently he had stumbled into the street just down the road from here and caused a motorbike accident."

"Well the app shows him at that hotel, is he there?"

"The lady at the front desk says she saw him about six but he hadn't been back all night."

"Holy shit!" Wasum said.

"Hang on, my friend just popped his head around the corner, he's motioning for me to come over", Decha said.

A few minutes passed. Wasum could hear shuffling footsteps and muffled voices.

"Decha, what's going on?"

"We found him. He's out cold. Looks pretty beat up. He's tucked away between a cargo truck and a cement wall. You'd never see him and wouldn't think to look for him back here."

"Is he ok?"

"My friend is going to talk to his friend at the front desk to see if we can sneak him in the back way and get him to his room."

"Oh my Buddha!" Wasum exhaled.

Decha's cohort came out the back way and propped the door open, saying "He's not even checked in here but she's going to let us use an employee meeting room on the second floor. We're going to get him up there on the freight elevator. She'll keep it under wraps for now but we need to get him out of here, fast. They'll find him eventually and probably throw him in jail."

Decha and his contact managed to get Willie up to the meeting room and assessed the situation from there. Willie was still out cold. Once up there they could see a big red mark on the side of his face and his clothes on the same side were scuffed and dirtied. He had a rip in his shirt with a little blood near his shoulder. They figured he hadn't been beaten up but had more likely fallen with a hell of a dead weight thud back behind that truck.

In a determined effort to rouse him from his stupor, they called out his name with increasing urgency, their voices rising in pitch. They shook him, trying to jolt him back to awareness. When that failed, they resorted to slapping his face, the sound of skin against skin echoing in the room. Still, he remained unresponsive. Desperation mounting, they dragged him into the bathroom and sprayed him with the shower hose letting the cold water hit his face in a relentless stream. Yet, despite their efforts, he remained oblivious, his chest rising and falling steadily, as if he were merely in a deep, unreachable slumber.

Decha's load out of Haneda back to Bangkok was scheduled to depart later that day. They figured the police would catch up to Willie before then, so they started scheming a way to sneak him out of there. All the way out. He wouldn't be safe in Tokyo, or anywhere in Japan.

Decha called Wasum and brought her up to speed.

"He's still out, and the police are bound to be closing in on him. We've got to get him out of town."

Wasum questioned, "Out of town?"

"Yes, out of town, out of Tokyo, out of Japan!" They'll throw the book at him if they catch up to him. The Japanese don't take kindly to Foreigners causing trouble over here. We found out one of the people on the motorbike, a local, had to go to the hospital after the wreck he caused."

"So what do we do? How the hell are you going to get him out of there?"

"I've got to somehow get him on that plane with me back to Bangkok. Once we're back on Thailand soil, everything gets easier."

"Ohhhhhhh," Willie groaned.

"That's a promising sign," Decha remarked. "Did you hear that?"

"Yes, I did," Wasum responded, while typing away on her laptop, attempting to reschedule a trip to Bangkok she had originally planned for February to an earlier date. "What about Thanaporn? Could she assist?"

Thanaporn was Decha and Wasum's cousin. She's a manager at a third-party contractor office in Bangkok that handles immigration and visa paperwork.

Decha and Wasum hail from a well-connected, affluent family with ties to the monarchy. Their family is well-known and influential enough to pull off a rescue plan in Thailand that could succeed, provided they managed to get Willie on that plane and out of Japan. So, they began plotting their strategy together.

Decha's contact was still in play, fascinated by the whole sordid affair. He would be instrumental in getting Willie to the plane. Once airborne, they'd be in the clear. All they needed was a convincing enough story and some paperwork that looked legitimate to fool a couple of lower-level security guards at BKK. They wouldn't have to deal with customs, just get past the gate guard—who would likely be known to Decha and relatively easy to deceive.

Willie, now barely aware of his surroundings, sees a man talking on a phone, his voice muted from the thunderous buzzing in his head. He barely made out…"Ok, you get a hold of Thanaporn. Have her put toge…" before it faded out completely as the man walked away towards the door to let someone in. Willie faded to black again.

Another few hours vanished. The front desk lady alerted Decha's connection that the police were checking all the hotels and were closing in. They were ready for the escape.

Straining to piece together fragments of his memory, Willie was now being partly dragged, partly walked out of the meeting room by two unfamiliar men. They guided him down the hallway. He was clueless about both what had transpired, and where he was being taken. One man loosened his grip with one hand while still holding firmly onto Willie's elbow with the other. He opened an old wooden hoistway door, and they entered a large freight elevator. Willie sensed they were descending. The elevator came to a stop, and they swiftly moved through a dimly lit corridor to a set of double doors. The light was blinding and disorienting as they passed through. A four-door truck awaited them, with a third man in the driver's seat. Willie and the two men holding him got into the back seat, and the truck sped off. The driver handed a legal-sized envelope and a small black travel bag to Decha. The man took some papers out of the envelope, glanced through them, muttered a few words in what might have been Japanese, and then placed the envelope into the bag.

The side of Willie's face was starting to throb by this time. He caught a glimpse of himself in the window as they approached the truck. He could see a bruise. He could feel the swelling. He had shooting pain in his right shoulder, ribs and hip.

Am I being abducted? he thought to himself.

Silence weighed heavily inside the truck, a tense quiet that seemed to amplify every bump and jolt. The driver maneuvered through the city streets with a relentless precision, as if on a mission handed down straight from the gods. Suddenly, they halted. Willie, trapped in a haze of disorientation and nausea, slipped back into a fog of semi-awareness. The vehicle's movements tossed him about, and the muffled drone of voices barely penetrated his consciousness before he slipped back into a void of oblivion.

Decha's contact vaulted into the front seat, leaving Decha and Willie in the back as they turned into the employee section of TIACT No. 1 International Cargo Building. The driver was a close ally of Decha's contact and held a senior position at the airport. With a swift, purposeful maneuver and a few waves to co-workers manning checkpoints along the way, he had whisked them all through the gate, navigating the facility's labyrinthine security with seamless precision. His mission: to deliver Decha to the prep area for the flight back to Bangkok, a delivery he had secured during his layover at Kansai.

"We've got 90 minutes before take-off. I need to do my prep," Decha stated, his voice steely with urgency. "Can you guys get Willie on the plane?"

"Yep."

"It's the Falcon on 1. Just tuck him in the jump seat behind the co-pilot. There's just one passenger. I'll cover the story. It should be fine."

With that, they whisked Willie away in a wheelchair, moving with military precision toward the plane. Willie, slipping in and out of various stages of confusion, mumbled incoherently, giving the men escorting him an indication he was still alive. As they approached the aircraft, they were abruptly halted by a stern security guard, his presence imposing and unyielding. The guard demanded to know their purpose. The driver of the truck, unwavering, presented his credentials with authority and declared they were executing a critical medical transport, destined for the charter jet just ahead. He pointed decisively to the Falcon, a sense of urgency pulsating through the air.

"Go ahead" the young guard said without even asking for any paperwork.

Upon reaching the plane, the men lifted Willie from the wheelchair and, with him groaning in pain, they partially carried and partially dragged him up the stairs.

"Where are you taking me?" he struggled to say.

"You'll be alright, Willie, Decha will take good care of you" one of them said.

With the aircraft ready, cargo onboard, and its sole passenger—a newly recruited flight attendant bound for Bangkok to begin her job with one of the charter companies Decha contracted with—they began to push back from the loading area.

"Who's that?" she asked.

"Medical transport," Decha replied.

"He doesn't look too good."

"No, he doesn't."

Once they received clearance for takeoff, the plane sped down the runway, lifted off smoothly, and just like that, they were headed up and out of Japanese airspace.

About thirty-minutes into the flight, Willie began to regain some awareness. He glanced around, noticed the fellow passenger seated behind him, heard the roar of the engines, and felt slight turbulence, and realized he was on an airplane. But where was it headed? Decha was seated diagonally from him at the controls, a co-pilot was directly in front of him, and that small black travel bag rested on his lap.

"Can I get a water?"

"Welcome back, Willie", Decha said as the co-pilot handed him back a cold water bottle. He drank nearly the whole thing in one swallow, then finished it off. The co-pilot handed him another.

"Bathroom?"

"In the back."

Willie stood up, wobbled, and sat back down.

"You ok?" Decha said.

"I'm ok."

After a few deep breaths that set his rib cage on fire, he slowly stood back up. As he made his way to the aft of the smaller aircraft—a Dassault Falcon 900— he noticed only two seats. The mid cabin was retrofitted for light cargo. There were two small secured pallets stacked on either side with boxes wrapped in plastic marked medical supplies. He forced a half smile to the young lady sitting in one of the seats as he walked by and found the door to the lavatory.

He pushed it open and stood at the sink, gripping its edges for support. As he splashed water on his face, each movement sent jolts through him, the cold liquid barely easing the sting of his skin. He looked at his reflection in the mirror and saw what a mean fight the hours, maybe days after his memory went dark had put up. A raw, purple shiner bloomed around his eye, and bruising spread like a storm over his cheekbone. His face was an abstract canvas of swelling and discoloration. Throbbing pain pulsed down from his shoulder, wrapping around his ribs like a vice. He felt each heartbeat like a hammer, tapping insistently against the sore flesh.

He took a moment to steady himself, tracing the unfamiliar geography of injuries with a grimace before turning to the narrow space behind him. Struggling slightly, he opened the door and stumbled back into the aisle. The plane shook gently, and he grabbed onto the seat back for support, the movement rattling his already rattled bones. He felt lightheaded, as if every bruise and throbbing muscle had taken on a weight all its own, dragging him down with each step. The low hum of the engines vibrated through his body, and he focused on that sound like a lifeline.

As he made his way back he asked the woman,

"Mind if I sit down?"

"Sure, go ahead"

He winced as he lowered himself into the empty seat across from her.

"What the hell happened to you?"

"Honestly, I have no idea."

"Must have been quite a party", she replied.

"It sure must have been."

He reclined his seat, put his head back and laid there trying again to remember what had happened.

"Where are we headed" he asked.

"Bangkok"

"Of course we are", he muttered.

For the next few hours, Willie drifted in and out of dreamless sleep, occasionally jerking awake with a start, as if he were falling into a void. The last jolt convinced him to reposition his seat upwards, resting his head on a small pillow against the wall next to the window. Focused on the futility of finding a position that didn't hurt he sat there shifting relentlessly in his seat, occasionally standing up to stretch and moan. This was going to be a brutal flight.

Another few hours passed and they finally began their descent into Suvarnabhumi Airport, quietly gliding over the city like a feather. He stared out the window and started to contemplate what he would do with the open air he hoped he'd have in front of him when the cabin door opened. *Should I run*, he thought. *I don't know anyone in Bangkok. I don't even know what I'm doing here.* He still didn't know any of these people. Didn't know if they were helping him or if they were kidnapping him. Was he in danger? He wasn't sure and didn't want to engage with anyone until he could piece together at least some of his darkened memory.

He settled on a decision. He'd try to break away and find an authority figure to help him get somewhere known and safe so he could contact someone back home and begin to unravel his lost memory.

It was then that he realized he didn't have his phone. As he went for the small black travel bag that had accompanied him to see if he could find any clues, he stopped short noticing a silver wedding ring on his left ring finger, and a tattoo—some lettering in a foreign language— on the inside of his right forearm. *What the hell is this!* He thought to himself.

Decha hollered back, "Everyone strapped in? We'll be touching down in 10 minutes."

"Willie?"

"Ya"

"Stay close to us when we get to the gate, we'll get you through security and over to the train station. My Aunt will have a good meal and a place laid out for you to rest and recover. Her son Tuk will pick you up at the Sisaket station and will drive you out to the farm. She'll fill in as many blanks as she can. You'll have to fill in the rest as you go. You'll be in good hands."

Feeling somewhat reassured, Willie decided to abandon his plan to bolt. He figured he'd ride it out and see where it all landed.

They touched down like a dream, braked to a slow roll and eventually came to a stop.

The co-pilot turned the latch handle on the door and with a push it swung out and up, the stairs fell smoothly on pneumatic extensions to the ground and they deboarded. Decha found a wheelchair nearby and told Willie to climb in.

"I can walk", Willie said.

"Get in, It's better this way. Trust me" Decha said.

As soon as they passed into the cargo terminal, a security guard intercepted them, barking a question at Decha in rapid-fire Thai. The air bristled with tension as Decha and the guard volleyed words back and forth, the exchange crackling with urgency. Decha swiftly rummaged through the travel bag, extracting the necessary paperwork and thrusting it at the guard. The guard scrutinized the documents with a hawk-like intensity, then finally nodded in approval, clearing their path forward.

After enduring the grueling pain of the seven-hour flight, followed by the chaos of navigating the terminal, the clock now ticked past seven thirty in the evening. Decha, moving with purpose, escorted Willie to the train station—a distance that seemed about thirty minutes away. He purchased a ticket with decisive speed and drilled into Willie precise instructions on where to wait and which train to board. Pressing five 100 baht bills into Willie's hand, he urged him to grab a meal on the train, ensuring he was equipped for the journey ahead.

"The train will arrive soon enough, around 9:30. The journey to Sisaket takes about 9 to 10 hours. Even though you don't have a phone or a watch, make sure to keep track of the time. Around 6 am, be vigilant for Sisaket Station. The train will make a quick stop, so be ready to get off. Tuk will meet you there. He'll be looking for you."

Willie, still in a lot of pain, still confused and disoriented, had a rush of vulnerability, even gratitude flush over him. He stepped forward and hugged Decha.

"Thanks, Man."

"You're going to be ok. Answers will come. My Aunt will look out for you until you can sort it out. Take care, Willie."

It had been nearly twenty hours since this ordeal began. Now, slouched on a bench in the humid sprawl of Bangkok, waiting to board a train bound for Sisaket, he reached back for something solid—anything—and came up empty. Just a haze. Kyoto Station, four days earlier, was the last clear image he could conjure before his memory went dark, and even that flickered like a dream already halfway out the door. Still, despite the chaos, the dull ache behind his eyes, the absence of a phone, and the disorienting stack of unanswered questions, Willie felt an unsettling calm. As if he'd slipped between dimensions. Fallen off the map. Disappeared from time itself.

In the distance he could feel the rumble of the train approaching. He stood up, grabbed the travel bag and followed the others—who had been trying unsuccessfully not to stare at the motley sight of a man before them who looked like he'd been drug through hell and back—to the platform.

'Car 8 - Seat 12 Second Class A/C Sleeper' it read on the ticket. As he made his way to his seat he observed it wasn't a seat at all. It was the top bunk in a row of sleeper-like capsules running parallel with the aisle. *Capsule! Why did this word nearly jog loose a memory?* Now feeling one solid ache from head to toe, he had a hell of a time making his way up. Once he did he found a decent mattress, a pillow and a blanket, and a privacy curtain. He eased down and nested in for the long ride to Sisaket, *wherever in the hell that is...*

There was an undeniable sense of nostalgia wrapped up in the clatter of that long train ride, a romance in the rails that evoked a different era altogether. The rhythmic rumble of the wheels, the mournful blow of the horn, the gentle swaying motion that rocked him like an infant in a cradle—it all conjured a simpler time, a time before life became tangled in chaotic knots and war wounds sprouting like unwanted weeds. A time when destinations were mysteries to be savored, not dilemmas to be solved. Willie tucked the travel bag under the pillow behind his head for added support, feeling the low thrum of the tracks around him, and let the hum of the train carry him away from the chaos and into the comforting arms of oblivion. He surrendered himself to the moment, embraced the timelessness of it, trying to ignore the battle scars his body wore as a memory of contorted hours passed. Let the waking world and its confounding riddles wait. It was easy to get lost in the music of the rails, letting them sing away the confusion. He intended to forget about the world and its expectations, if only for a little while, and drift away into a place where the past and future ceased to exist, where only the present mattered.

As the small world around him disappeared, Willie slipped silently into another dreamless slumber, one so profound that it bordered on amnesia, erasing pain and doubt until they were less than shadows.

He didn't know how long he'd been out, only that time had lost its grip on him and the monotonous chaos of the past few days slowly dissolved into nothing, suddenly bringing him to a different kind of awareness.

Seven hours later he woke up to a perfectly still train in an unknown village in the dark of the Thailand sky. A little unsettling, barely a sound could be heard. He looked out the window and people filled the streets, carnival rides, elephant ears...*elephant ears? Am I reading that right?*, food vendors on both sides of the street. Yet, he couldn't hear a sound. It was surreal. He sat and watched through that window like he'd slipped into a parallel universe. Was it a dream? Was all of it a dream? The pain he was feeling in his body didn't jibe with that premise. Within a few minutes, the train roared back to life and continued its trek towards what would hopefully, soon, be Sisaket. After that weird sight, he wasn't sure.

Willie clumsily rolled out of his bunk, landed with a wince on the floor, grabbed his bag and set off in search of a bathroom and some food. After walking through about eight cars forward, he finally reached the dining car. Only two other people were there, enjoying an ice cream cone. His eyes caught sight of the bar at the front—his instincts were still sharp, thankfully—and he headed over to check it out. An ice cooler was filled with large, cold, dewy cans of Chang beer, Leo beer, and Heineken. He pointed to the Leo, handed the bartender one of the bills Decha had given him, then another after a grin and soft point to his hand for more, and when the bartender tried to return some coins, Willie gestured for her to keep them. She smiled in response. With his big, cold can of Leo beer in hand, he left the glass she offered at the bar, walked back to a booth at the rear of the car, and popped the can open. That beer was colder and tasted better than any he'd ever remembered. He finished it, ordered a second, and sat back down.

He'd been carrying this confounding small black travel bag ever since Tokyo, without even realizing it. In perpetual distraction he never had a chance to peek inside. While sitting there, halfway through his second Leo, he unzipped the bag, retrieved a legal-sized envelope, and placed it on the table in front of him. A quick glance back inside the bag revealed toiletries: deodorant, toothpaste, a toothbrush, a travel pack of Q-tips, lotion, and a small pack of tissues with Japanese writing on the package. "Huh," he remarked aloud, finding it amusing.

He opened the flap of the envelope, turned it over— his passport fell out—and took out the papers. There were about a half dozen letter size sheets of paper with Thai writing, some both sides, tables with checks and handwritten scribbles and signatures, and some with official looking red inked stamps. He examined them closely. One looked like a certificate, the type you receive after completing a course. Most of the text was in Thai, except for his name, Willie James Lyonsan. The scribble beneath seemed to be a name as well, with the last name matching his—Lyonsan. He decided to show it to the bartender.

"What is this?" The document was a puzzle piece that begged for context.

The bartender leaned in, her eyes scanning the paper with the quick expertise of someone accustomed to translating chaos for foreigners.

"Looks like a marriage license," she said, as casually as if she'd been asked about the weather.

He sat back down. A marriage license? Each syllable reverberated, setting off a cascade of new questions that collided with the old ones. He ran a hand over his stubbly head, trying to smooth down the mental static. *A marriage license? Who the hell did I marry? And why can't I remember?* He thought to himself.

The name on the document, the same as his own, taunted him with its possibility.

He wondered who the hell *he* really was now.

Before Willie could dig deeper into this new layer of confusion, the train came to an abrupt halt and soon after a shadow loomed over him, startling him back into the immediacy of the moment.

"Sisaket", an official looking fellow barked, followed by some rumblings in Thai he couldn't understand.

"Thanks", Willie said as he stuffed the papers back into the envelope, back into the bag, and headed for the door. He got off the train.

The sun was coming up. The sky was glowing a bright yellow/orange at the horizon. The town was mostly silent. The platform was quiet too and devoid of anything other than the small handful of people who got off the train from different cars, and they had already dispersed into bathrooms or waiting cars. As he stood there alone he looked over at the makeshift, tin roofed market stands that lined the other side of the tracks in one direction, and the small water tower that was almost completely overgrown with vegetation in the other when he heard the latch on a chain link gate clang behind him. He turned around to see a young man, late teens-early twenties, maybe, heading his way. He walked up to greet him with a big toothy smile.

"Tuk?"

"Ka" he grunted with a little throaty laugh, smile still plastered to his face.

"How's it going", Willie said. Tuk didn't respond, just kept smiling. Willie soon figured out this kid didn't know a single word of english.

They made their way back through the chain link gate, across a small lawn and into a parking lot to a small, bluish, early 90's Toyota Hilux fitted with a cab and a half. Tuk grabbed Willie's bag and they both went for the right side door. Tuk shot him a puzzled look.

"Thought I was aiming for the passenger side", Willie chuckled

Pointing at the steering wheel. "You guys drive on the right side here, eh?"

No reply, Tuk just smiled. He went around to the other side and got in.

It was an uneventful ride. Tuk inched along with caution at a mind numbing, snail's pace, cars whizzing by as if they were stationary road art. He never uttered a sound. Willie talked to himself much of the way, intrigued by the new surroundings.

"Oh that's a pretty lake. Check out that rice field. I can't believe how many dogs are roaming around. What the hell is that", to a strange, skinny contraption that resembled an elongated rototiller chopper hitched to a wagon.

On this, his inaugural journey through the lush Thailand countryside, he was mesmerized by the sights of more motorbikes than he'd encountered in his entire life. Families of up to four, wedged in one behind another, zipping down the narrow streets with a fearless urgency, as if being chased by the wind. Along the roadside, serene monks in saffron robes ambled with a tranquil grace, while towering, resplendent golden Buddhas gazed over the landscape, embodying peace and majesty. Magnificent temples, adorned with intricate carvings and vibrant colors, stood as testaments to devotion and artistry. Adding to the countryside's unique tapestry were the curious rototiller contraptions, their engines tek tek tek'ing along as they hauled bountiful crops, hinting at the region's deep-rooted agricultural life. There were beautiful forestlands with perfectly rowed trees that seemed to stretch endlessly towards the edge of the world.

They traveled through village after village until they approached a picturesque farm that seemed to be the heart of yet another small village. Unlike the houses he'd seen on the journey from Sisaket, this gated home was larger, more elegant, meticulously maintained, with a veranda and an enclosed porch. The atmosphere was serene, complete with well-kept outbuildings, chickens darting around, water buffalo grazing across vast, endless fields, and impressive machinery—everything you could imagine.

As they approached, a distinguished gentleman, seemingly plucked straight from the pages of a Hollywood movie script, looked at Willie with a smile, pressed his palms together and bowed. He then engaged in a brief conversation with Tuk. Their laughter rang out, genuine and hearty, with broad smiles lighting up their faces. Tuk glanced down at the freshly cut grass, his head shaking slightly in amusement, a grin still firmly in place.

Another few minutes passed as Willie stood there, trying to absorb everything like a dry sponge in a rainstorm. The morning sun stretched long shadows over the lawn, and just when the anticipation reached its peak, a pretty woman emerged from the direction of the house, striding confidently across the freshly cut grass with three water bottles in hand. Her long black hair flowed like silk behind her, dancing in time with each step. She walked in their direction, and her expression was unreadable—a mix of purpose and playfulness that he couldn't quite pin down. She was petite, graceful, and had a presence that seemed to fill the entire space between them. Who was she? The old mans wife? Daughter? Another woman, younger, emerged behind her. Quickening her gate she trailed behind the first woman by ten or so paces, closing the gap rapidly. As she was coming into focus, he heard a familiar voice.

"Willie, oh my god I can't believe you're here."

He leaned forward just a hair, brows knitting as he squinted in the direction of the voice, "Wasum!?" he blurted out, "What the fuck are you...ooof!" Willie nearly fell over from the collision of Wasum's clumsy lurch in to hug him. "Careful, careful", he winced. "What's going on, what are you doing here?" he questioned.

And then he heard...

"Welcome to Thailand, Win," from a voice that sent a shiver down his spine, one he eerily recognized. The familiarity of it was unsettling, almost ghostly. It couldn't be... His heart pounded as he spun around quickly, the hair on his neck standing on end, prickling with a mix of anticipation and disbelief. The humid air seemed to thicken around him, and the bustling sounds of the farm faded into the background.

"Chitra!"

Disoriented, spent, and utterly blindsided, he needed to sit before gravity did the job for him. Desperately, he sank to the ground, his body collapsing against a cluster of large bundled rice stalks, his heart pounding, seemingly, out of his chest...

"I knew you'd make it home one day, Win…" Chitra said with a coy smile, her voice soft with wonder.

Scene 2

Meet Willie Lyonsan

You don't meet a man like Willie Lyonsan and forget him. He doesn't walk into your life so much as drift into it, like a song you've never heard but somehow already know the words to. He's not the loudest in the room, not always the first to speak—often the last—but somehow the gravity shifts when he shows up. And before you know it, he's at the center of things—laughing, storytelling, making everyone feel like they've just remembered who they really are.

Willie's the kind of guy who'll drive an hour out of his way to fix your screen door, just because he was "already sort of headed that way" (he wasn't). He's the one who remembers your mom's name, your dog's name, and the song that was playing when you said you didn't believe in love anymore. He's a walking contradiction—fiercely independent, yet endlessly loyal; equal parts poet, mechanic, philosopher, and stray dog.

My old pal Willie Lyonsan and I have been in lockstep since we were five years old, a couple of kids with the bounds of madness and the energy to match. We meshed as if cast from the same mold, getting on like a house on fire from day one, our friendship a force of nature. We'd spend the bulk of our time marauding around our little neighborhood in Beaverton, Michigan, an idyllic Midwest farming town replete with endless rolling cornfields, old centennial farms, hunting, fishing, a local grainery and a small-town square adjacent to the Tastee Freeze.

Fitzgerald Square was the hub of all things Beaverton, from the annual traveling amusement park—featuring the tilt-a-whirl, zipper, and bumper cars—to 4H fundraisers and weekend antique tractor shows. Our childhood orbit revolved around these quintessential locales, each season bringing its own events and characters. Like a couple of feral miscreants, we'd shoot marbles and BBs beneath the wooden bleachers at the Little League diamond, race around like daredevils in or on any manner of loud and wheeled apparatus we could cobble together, or dare each other to climb and conquer the towering hay bales barned up beyond the fields. Our world was vast and important, a swath of open land and free spirit.

Summer was our time, and we wore it down to a nub. Days stretched like the horizon, bookended by our mothers' calls to return, always ignored in favor of our games and imaginings. Willie and I forged our adventures in what felt like the center of the universe but was, in truth, a nothing speck on the map, tucked away from the rest of life's chaos. Our childhood was a paean to innocence, each moment a capsule of pure escapism. As kids, the world seemed infinite, and so did we within it.

We never tired; we never stopped. We'd scour the mighty stacks of corn for raccoons while the smell of earth and growing things clung to our sneakers and lingered in the air. Hours were spent plotting the construction of subterranean forts, Willie masterminding the scheme and me following his blueprints with the loyalty of a half-starved hound. It was a grand theater, and we were nothing short of maestros. Even on school nights, we savored the last light like it might be our last, our bikes careening through the unpaved scrub and gravel lots like the goddamn Tour de

France, our clothes speckled with dirt and unchecked laughter.

Winter brought its own rituals, the sledding hills, ice hockey on the pond, and never-ending snowball fights that turned us into warriors against the blizzard backdrop. But it was in summer that we found magic. Summer was ours by birthright. We knew every inch of Beaverton by heart, every back alley and dirt path, the forgotten orchards and the places where time seemed to stop and let us pass. Nothing could stop us or slow us down, not even the threat of sunburns or chores or bickering siblings. It was adventure on demand, and we took full advantage.

"Willie, you and Oscar come in for lunch now" Willie's mom would holler out the door. Forever wanting to stay outside we'd run in like a couple of bandits, grab the paper plates of peanut butter and jelly sandwiches and chips on the counter and fly right back out the door.

I may have mentioned some of this before, but it bears repeating with some extra detail because it all shaped who Willie was, who he became, where he went, and how he got there. My folks bought the house across the street from Willies. Both his great grandmothers lived next door to us and next door to Willie's were his Grandparents on his Dad's side. It was utopian for Willie. For me too! Most evenings we'd be over at "the Grandma's" eating vanilla ice cream with spooned over Hershey's syrup watching Lawrence Welk, Andy Griffith, or Roy Clark and Minnie Pearl on Hee-Haw. Behind the Grandma's house were two giant blueberry bushes. Blackberries, raspberries and rhubarb grew in the side yard. Mouthwatering homemade pies were a weekly delight.

Even back then, there was an enigmatic aura that surrounded Willie, like he was a time traveler with a suitcase full of wisdom from yesteryears. He seemed to possess an old soul, one that wasn't easily swayed by the whims of the present or the fleeting trends that captured the attention of others. Willie marched to the rhythm of his own drum, indifferent to society's ever-changing tempo.

When we were nine, his parents split up, an event that sent ripples through his young life. His sister Annie, four years his senior—his steadfast confidante, even to this day—confided in me that the divorce left him reeling, a tempest in his heart. The devastation was profound, and in a desperate attempt to shield his fragile spirit, he buried the pain deep within, never allowing it to surface. His parents and extended family did their best to cushion the blow, maintaining holiday traditions and being a constant presence in Willie and his sister's lives. But the rupture left an indelible mark on Willie, shaking him to his very core. This added a new layer of complexity to his worldview, undoubtedly sowing a few of the seeds for the long list of misadventures that trailed him throughout his life, like a shadow that refused to be shaken.

Willie's entire family was immersed in creative pursuits. His Dad and Grandpa were his heroes—traditional typesetters who ran an offset printing shop with his Uncle. Willie spent a lot of time there thinking to the rhythm of the presses and drinking in the scent of the ink. He adored that place. His Mom, his rock, was a writer, and his aunts, uncles, cousins, and even his sister were all talented musicians. After the divorce, both of his parents remarried fairly quickly—his Dad to a graphic designer and his Mom to a luthier.

Informed by all the angst and open beauty a family of creatives brings, Willie moved through life like a social chameleon with a moral compass wired to empathy instead of convention. His circle—if you could even call it that—was less of a shape and more of a swirl: misfits, criminals, professors, hustlers, musicians, and entrepreneurs. He had a gift, almost otherworldly, for making fast, genuine connections across every social strata imaginable—always slipping in like he'd been there all along.

He once struck up a conversation with an older Black woman sitting alone in a Detroit hospital waiting room. He was there visiting a friend who had gotten into a car accident. Her son, as it turned out, had just been shot—a high-level drug dealer known to all the right (and wrong) people in the city. Willie didn't know that. He just saw a woman in pain and sat with her. Talked to her. Listened. Made her laugh a little, forget the weight of the world for a moment. That was his magic.

Before the night was over, she hugged him like kin and told him he was coming to an upcoming family barbecue. And he did—joyfully. Showed up wind blown from the ride on his beloved Kawasaki with a bottle of Glenlivet 12-year and a smile wide enough to crack pavement. He was the only white face there, and yet somehow it didn't matter. They embraced him. Willie belonged.

That chance meeting spun into years of connection. He ran with that family—clubs, cookouts, birthdays, court dates. He'd pull up to gatherings in neighborhoods you and I wouldn't dare step foot in, and be greeted like a cousin back from college. And when the son—her boy—was eventually arrested, tried, and sentenced to thirty years, Willie was right there in the courtroom gallery. Starkly out of place by every conventional measure, and yet somehow woven perfectly into the fabric of the moment. Just another thread in the tapestry.

Willie has a heart of gold and nary a speck of ill-intention. He could downplay the worst scenarios with a crooked grin and a chuckle, as if chaos itself were just another errand to run before lunch. There's something about that energy—some strange alchemy in the way he refused to panic—that seemed to bend the laws of consequence. Disasters that would wreck most men simply… evaporated around him. He wasn't the guy who fell into a pile of shit and came out smelling like a rose—no, he came out covered in it, grinning, offering you a hug, and somehow you ended up feeling lucky for the encounter. It wasn't clean, but it was charmed in its own way. And what came out the other side of most of his tumbles? More often than not, it led to something unexpected. Something meaningful. A strange new friendship, a life lesson mended in duct tape, or a door kicked open to the next wild chapter. Trouble didn't break Willie. It built him—one dented, ridiculous, unforgettable story at a time.

Willie had the air of a man who'd been places—important places. The kind of swagger that suggested a prestigious education, martini boardrooms, and a contact list full of politicians and rockstars. He carried himself like someone who had the world by the short hairs and wasn't particularly worried about losing his grip. You couldn't help but like the guy. But the truth, if you peeled back the layers, wasn't even close. Willie was a high school dropout with a string of failed ventures stacked behind him like empty soup cans tied to the bumper of a just-married car. No pot to piss in, no window to throw it out of. Owned but one thing outright—the Kawasaki KZ900 he'd traded a car stereo for back in high school. He refused to part with it. It was his soul and his solace. And still, somehow, he floated through the world like it owed him something beautiful—and often, it paid up.

Willie much preferred two wheels to four, open air in his face to a windshield. Did a lot of his thinking behind handlebars. He had an IQ hovering around 140, not that he ever mentioned it. In fact, he had a knack for making everyone else feel like the smartest person in the room. It wasn't a trick. It was empathy, pure and simple. Willie had this almost eerie ability to become the mirror of whoever he was talking to—whether it was a billionaire on a golf course or a broken soul on a barstool. He'd lock in, nod once or twice, offer a word or two that somehow cut to the marrow, and if you were down on your luck, he might slip you a few bucks he didn't really have. Never for credit. Just because.

He'd always been that way. Ever since we were kids, Willie was the rescuer, the healer. Back then, the stakes were low—a scraped knee, a broken bike chain, a bruised ego. But adulthood raised the price of admission. The people who needed saving were heavier, and the cost to carry them left a mark. Sometimes he carried too many for too long. And yet, Willie seemed immune to despair. He treated each morning like a blank page, like none of the heartache or financial train wrecks from the day before had any jurisdiction over today. The man had a short memory for personal loss— whether that was a blessing or a curse, I never could figure out. But I do know this: Willie loved with his whole chest, gave until it hurt, and never once looked for the receipt.

Willie had a fondness for drinking and quite a thing for Whiskey. He never got hooked, not by a long shot. He just loved the whole ceremony of being out with people, laughing and swapping stories. He got started young, 13 or maybe 14. He'd sneak a taste from his Grandpa's Jim Beam stash—the ones with those wildlife pictures by James Lockhart. He'd never break a seal, he'd just swipe a bit from the ones already open. But he quickly got a real knack for top-notch whiskey, Scotch too. His dad only stocked the good stuff. His first Scotch was a 14-year Balvenie, probably older than him at the time. His first bourbon—a dusted off bottle of George Dickel #12. When his pals would sneak a flask of Evan Williams or Old Crow from their dad's stash, he'd take a drink, spit it out, and shout, "That stuff makes my teeth itch!"

Willie loved his beer, too, though he never got into the premiums of the day—Lowenbrau or Heineken—or the craft brews of today. His preference lay with the classics, the great American lagers. Hamm's was his favorite, Old Style, Pabst, Strohs. He would always enjoy sharing a few beers with friends, but he saw beer more as a nice accompaniment to whiskey. Not a chaser, mind you. Perish the thought. He would order a whiskey alongside a can of beer, taking only the occasional sip from the latter. A few whiskeys in, he might have an empty can and be ready for another. I never saw Willie drunk, drunk as in *drunk as a skunk*. Never saw him lose his cool or roll without restraint. Infectiously cheerful when sober, the more he drank, the more cheerful he became. He'd get funnier, too, as the night wore on. And, as you might have guessed, he's already pretty damn funny sober.

Willie is what you might call the quintessential good-time Joe—the life of the party, always. People lit up when he arrived, leaned in when he spoke, and laughed harder than they had in weeks just being near him. He carried a kind of chaotic charisma, the kind that made even his train wrecks sound like bucket-list adventures. Like the time he ran off to Vegas with the exotic dancer from Kentucky. That one's a dandy. Or the French-African blues singer he dated—the one who tried to run him off the road in a high-speed chase after spotting him with another woman tucked too close beside him. Then there's the time he started throwing peanuts out his window at a patched biker at a red light, thinking it was his buddy, just to impress the girl next to him. It wasn't his buddy. Or the time he called a Native woman whose photo he spotted on an event flyer—just cold-called her to ask her out—only to learn she lived a thousand miles and three states away. "So instead of this evening, tomorrow then," he said, cool as ice. Amused, she accepted. And off he and Lou went. He stayed three days.

I'll circle back to Lou a little later. You won't want to miss that.

Willie never belonged anywhere, not really. Beaverton couldn't hold him. The place was too small for the way his mind wandered, too quiet for the songs he hummed under his breath. Colorado, Wyoming, South Dakota, Alabama— he'd lived in a lot of places, each one leaving a mark but still never quite fit. But Arizona... Arizona was different. Cave Creek, specifically. He spent nearly fifteen years there, and it was the closest he ever came to feeling anchored. The people he met weren't just friends—they nested in his soul, etched themselves deeper than blood. That dusty little town wrapped itself around him in a way no place ever had before. And yet, he still couldn't shake that ache he had inside to go. It wasn't really so much a pull inside him to go as it was a calling—something ancient, cosmic even. Like the universe itself had cupped its hands around his spirit and whispered, *Come see what I've made for you.* It was a plea, really. Not a tug from within, but a ringing from without—reverberating in his bones, impossible to ignore.

He was raised on a steady diet of other people's dreams—books stacked like bricks, music bleeding through thin walls, stories told in the hush of night by artists and craftsmen and eccentrics who'd never once followed a map. His mother wrote. His stepdad built guitars. His aunt painted like her soul had been lit on fire and her only relief was canvas. Willie absorbed it all. And when he found cameras—when he got behind the lens—it was like he'd found a sixth sense.

He never took a picture for money. Hated the idea of mixing commerce with art. But he'd shoot a rusted-out tractor in a dying cornfield and somehow make it feel like it had a story to tell. Same with portraits. Maybe especially with portraits. Willie could look through a lens and catch the exact frame where someone let their guard down, just for a second. That's what he chased—not perfection, but the truth buried in the shadows, inside the mess.

But if you're thinking all this makes him some enlightened guru with a monk's sense of peace, let me stop you right there. Willie's not a saint. He's got a long history of chasing the wrong things for the right reasons, or maybe the right things for the wrong reasons—it's never been clear. He's burned bridges, ghosted good people, and left more than a few messes for others to clean up. But none of it comes from malice. It's that restless spirit. The kind that doesn't understand comfort as a destination. The kind that keeps packing and unpacking bags because *somewhere* must be calling.

He's got a soft spot for misfits and underdogs. The broken, the loud, the forgotten. Willie has this radar for pain —like he can sniff it out from across the room. And instead of turning away like most folks do, he moves toward it. Not to fix it, exactly, but to sit with it. A silent witness, never judging. I think that's why people open up to him so easily. They sense, without understanding how, that Willie won't just hear them—he'll carry a piece of their story with him. He always has.

And Willie loves big. Not in some sweep-you-off-your-feet, Hallmark kind of way. No, his love is messier than that. It's chaotic and stubborn and fierce. It's staying up all night to fix your car because he overheard you say you were nervous about driving it. It's showing up to your court date even though you never asked. It's staying far too long in relationships that devour him because he believes—really believes—that he can carry someone else's darkness if it means they'll feel a little more light.

I've watched this man give away everything—his money, his time, his peace of mind. And not once have I seen him regret it. He carries his heartbreaks like heirlooms, wraps them in flannel and tucks them into the glove box. They're part of the ride. He doesn't forget them, but he doesn't stop driving either.

You know, there's a moment from years ago I can't get out of my head. We were at some crummy bar on the edge of town—Me, Willie, Louie and a handful of locals half in the bag by 7 p.m. all lining the bar. Willie struck up a conversation with a janitor, a wiry guy with nicotine-stained fingers and a face like sandpaper. They talked about nothing —tools, ball bearings, maybe a bit about jazz. But by the end of the night, Willie knew the man's whole life story: two kids, one estranged, one incarcerated. And when the guy's eyes welled up mid-sentence, Willie didn't flinch. Just leaned in, offered him his whiskey, and said, "Yeah, man. Life's a bastard sometimes, ain't it?" I watched that janitor look at him like he was Moses parting the Red Sea. No one before had probably bothered talking to him.

That's the thing with Willie. He doesn't preach. Doesn't hand out answers. He just shows up. And somehow, that's enough. People are drawn to him like moths to a neon beer sign—buzzing close, lingering too long, always warmed by the glow. He's made fast friends in a dozen zip codes, earned trust in places he barely belonged, and seemed to leave behind stories in every booth, barstool, and borrowed couch he ever passed through. But if there was one soul who ever truly got him—saw past the charm and the sidelong grin, past the soft-sell rebellion and disheveled genius—it was a 40-pound Boston Bull named Louie. Louie didn't ask questions. He didn't need explanations. He just watched Willie with those steady, stone-set eyes and loved him exactly as he was: reckless, radiant, unfinished.

Yeah, ol' Willie might be hard to pin down. Maybe he loses interest too fast, or disappears for long stretches, or quits just as things are getting good. But if you've ever had a friend like that—someone who knows you even when you forget yourself—you understand why people stay in his orbit. You understand why I stayed.

Willie Lyonsan is flawed, fallible, and frustrating as hell. But I swear to you, when you've been lucky enough to walk beside him, even for a little while, the world looks different. A little more alive. A little more worth saving.

And that's why I followed him all the way to Thailand. That's why I'm telling this story.

Because when Willie disappears off the map—and he always does—you start to wonder what part of yourself might've gone with him.

Scene 3

A Sijo, and Kentucky

My best friend, Willie Lyonsan—lover of women, bad decisions, and new zip codes—was married four times in as many states. If there's a record for interstate romantic chaos, he may hold it. And no two of those unions were anything alike, except for the fact that each one ended exactly how you'd expect if you knew Willie: in flames, dust, or a dramatic, whiskey-fueled getaway.

Some people marry for love. Some for money. Some for visas. Willie? Willie has married on a dare, to settle a bet, and once just for a place to hang his hat.

The latter was his first. He was barely twenty one, living out of his car in an ungodly nowhere town outside

Battle Creek, Michigan. There was this quiet little side road that ran from the gravel patch beside the shrub line—where he'd tuck away his old, beat-up Pontiac LeMans—to the dive bar he frequented almost daily. Seemed he'd always sniff out the nearest dive bar wherever he was. Every night on the way there he'd pass this one house, a modest, slightly run down two-story with plastic flowers out front and a porch light that flickered like morse code.

The woman who lived there was Korean, 38 years old, who worked at the factory in town, like most others living there. She had a cold look and a no-nonsense aura that made most men cross to the other side of the street. Not Willie. He tipped his hat every night like some dusty cowboy, calling out, "Good evening, Miss." She was quite beautiful if you looked through the snarl. After a few weeks, she finally asked him in very broken English what he was doing sleeping in his car like a stray dog. He gave her that Willie grin and shrugged, "It's home."

"Well don't park it there, park it here on my side of the shrubs...you'll eventually get it towed parking there", she barked.

He circled back, jumped in, cranked it over, wheeled it around and in less than a minute, it was parked on her side of the shrubs, safe and sound. He got out of the car, glanced back, tipped his hat and hollered out "Thanks a lot" with a wave, and off to the tavern he went.

Her name was Hui Ko. She had three kids—13, 16, 19 —and worked ten-hour shifts at the local textile plant around the corner. She'd been living there on her own for quite a few years. Her ex-husband, who also worked at the plant, had been a US soldier stationed in Korea. He married her there and brought her back. Within five or six years he left her for a local girl—one his mother approved of—to fend for herself.

She was well-liked in town. She'd make big trays of egg-rolls—I'm talking authentic, world-class, straight from the mother-country variety—and smartly drop them off in batches at the town hall for the clerk, police and fire staff, and she'd give them away to neighbors and local businesses. Shortly after her husband left her she walked to the textile plant. The shift supervisor was a regular recipient of her famous egg rolls through his wife. She asked him for a job. He obliged. She went to work the following week. She worked first shift. Her ex-husband worked second. It seemed to work.

Behind where Willie parked his car and down the hill there was a rather large overgrown garden that had seen better days. Willie asked her about it. She said she used to grow all of her own vegetables there but when her husband left she didn't have the time. Willie borrowed the neighbors rototiller one day while Hui Ko was at work and tilled that whole garden. Planted corn, lettuce, tomatoes, potatoes, peppers and a few other vegetables over the following few days. She was thrilled. Willie tended that garden like a man trying to coax forgiveness from the dirt.

She'd bring him water and meals. He'd be out there working away for hours on end. The garden came in nicely. This was a good arrangement.

With Willie, though, good arrangements were usually followed by some unintended chaos fueled by a sequence of inexplicable events.

As time went on, the routine seemed set. Willie would drum up day work somewhere, come *home* to his little patch at Casa de LeMans, tend the garden, and head out to the tavern. Week in. Week out.

By now, fall was in the air. The garden's harvest was pretty well wrapped up and the nights carried with them a chill that required an extra blanket or two to get through. Hui Ko knew this. She and Willie didn't have anything physical going on between them. Just a friendship, of sorts. He genuinely liked her and she grew to genuinely like him. They'd drink beer together on lawn chairs by the garden sometimes after dinner. They had a few laughs. She could see he was a pretty good guy with a pretty good heart. After being alone for so long, it was nice to have a guy around to help out. He never interacted with her kids. Pok the oldest was nearly Willie's age. They had their own lives. To them, Willie was just the weird guy who lived in his car behind the garage.

One night after drinking a few beers together, and probably a few shots of whiskey, Hui Ko, a woman with fiercely traditional Korean standards, made an off-hand suggestion. "It's getting cold at night, you want to sleep inside now? If you do, you have to marry me first though!", she exclaimed in a loud, broken, animated tone.

"Ok." Willie replied.

Three days later, they were married.

Willie grabbed his pillow, blanket and bathroom bag and moved into the house. Snug as a bug in a rug...

Hui Ko's kids weren't thrilled. They looked at Willie like a fungus growing under the sink. The eldest, Pok, was only two years younger than Willie, which made for one hell of a dynamic. It started off rocky—side-eyes, slammed doors, silent meals—but Willie had a gift. He was magnetic in a way you couldn't explain. Pretty soon, they all came around and really got to like him. Willie wasn't the greatest influence on

Pok, who soon started ditching school assignments—he attended the local college—and day drinking stolen Soju with Willie while Hui Ko was hard at work, none the wiser...

Needless to say, the honeymoon phase didn't last very long.

But the beginning of the end came on what was supposed to be a routine delivery run. Willie scored a gig delivering premium wholesale roses to a distributor down in Kentucky, not far over the Indiana border. Twelve-hours round trip. Easy money. Leave at noon, drop the load by five, grab a quick bite and gas up, be home in time to buy a round at the tavern and tell another tale. Simple.

Only, on *that* particular day, Pok showed up around 10 a.m. with a bottle of Jim Beam and two corn dogs. "Breakfast of champions," he said. And that's how the trouble began.

They drank in the garage until Willie's vision got a little wide. Pok bet him he couldn't do the delivery and be back in less than ten hours. Willie took the bet. Got behind the wheel of the clunky old delivery van he was assigned— the one with a busted odometer and loose gas gauge— and with forty bucks in his pocket and what he *thought* was a full tank of gas, off he went.

Around 4:40 p.m., twenty minutes from his drop-off, the engine sputtered and died. He coasted onto the shoulder, cursed the universe, and looked up to see a flickering neon sign just down the street: *Puss N Boots Gentleman's Club.*

Willie took it as a divine message.

Inside, the air was thick with perfume and bad decisions. He sat at the bar, ordered a boilermaker, and tried to act like he belonged. And that's when he saw her.

Lexi. A redhead with fire in her step and brass in her soul. Five foot nothing, attitude for days, a voice like broken glass and velvet. She didn't dance. She commanded.

Willie was smitten. He sat through her whole set like it was Shakespeare. She noticed him too—this strange, charming drifter in scuffed boots and a beat-up Carhartt jacket. When her shift ended, she sat beside him, swiped his drink, and asked if he believed in fate.

They talked until closing, then until sunrise. She told him about her dream of moving to Vegas and opening a tattoo parlor for bikers. He told her about his epic gardening skills and his ongoing feud with a neighborhood rooster named Jerry.

By now, his goose was thoroughly cooked back at home. Hui Ko would be absolutely livid. He was supposed to have returned by 11, or midnight at the very latest, and here it was 6 am the next morning. The delivery was never completed—the load of roses lay blown and wilted in the back of the van, which still sat abandoned on the side of the road. His boss would surely have his hide for this blunder.

Most of Willie's misadventures—especially the later, more operatic ones—usually came by way of a wrong turn he didn't mean to take, or a series of unforeseen events that derailed whatever half-decent intentions he might've started with. But not this one. No, this one was different. This one was on Willie. Squarely.

Granted, he was only twenty-one at the time—young, broke, and still figuring out what not to do with his life. But still. He had a weakness. Developed it early. Women. The moment one got within fifty feet of his gravitational pull, his emotional radar would short-circuit. It'd flicker and tumble like an old ceiling fan on its last leg—wobbling, groaning, rattling itself loose until the whole damn thing tore free and crashed to the floor in a spectacular mess of sparks and bad decisions.

So now what? He was in it deep. Married to Hui Ko— basically for the roof—and now caught with his pants metaphorically (and maybe literally) down. He'd disappeared for a delivery job, never called, never showed back up, and spent the night wrapped up in Lexi, a redheaded fireball who was currently chain-smoking and daring him to run off to Vegas.

Said they could stay with her sister. Said she was leaving anyway. Said the universe was giving them a sign.

Willie paced a little in his head. Going back wasn't much of an option. Hui Ko would kill him—slowly. His boss would surely dock him pay he didn't have for the roses he never delivered. That left one door wide open.

Vegas, huh? He thought to himself.

What the hell. When you start with nothing, it's easy to start over. Again.

He'd need to gas up the van, make one quiet run back to the house while Hui Ko was at work, sneak in, grab a few things, grab the LeMans, and burn rubber westward. That was the plan.

"I'm in," Willie said.

"In what?" Lexi asked, looking at him sideways.

"Vegas," he grinned. "Let's do it."

Lexi grabbed a couple garbage bags' worth of essentials from her apartment, chucked them in the back of the van, told her roommate she was gone for good, and just like that, they were off.

Northbound, directionless, high on adrenaline and low on gas—headed for the shimmering mirage that was Las Vegas, Nevada.

As they approached town, they kept to the back roads —narrow veins of cracked pavement flanked by cornfields and low-slung power lines. They crept around the edge of town like burglars casing a joint. Willie took a winding route through dirt-road neighborhoods, avoiding main streets, avoiding chance run-ins, avoiding fate.

Then came Acorn—the textile plant where Hui Ko worked. Willie caught sight of her car in the lot out of the corner of his eye as they passed.

Good. She was at work. Game on.

He took the turn onto the narrow side road where he used to park. Rolled the van slow over the gravel patch beside the shrub line, just like old times. So far, so good. Lexi stayed behind, tossing her bags into the LeMans and sliding into the passenger seat without a word—like she'd done it a hundred times.

Willie crept around the garage, moving like a fox in church shoes, and made his way to the side door. Quietly, he slid it open and slipped inside. The house was still. Empty. Just the low hum of the fridge and a TV someone forgot to turn off. He didn't need much. A couple changes of clothes.

His bathroom bag. Maybe the books on his nightstand if he had time.

But something felt... off. This was too easy.

He moved quick. Grabbed what he needed and made for the door. Swung it open, and all he saw was blinding daylight between him and the LeMans. Lexi—looking like a goddamn accomplice in a getaway scene—was motioning out her rolled down window for Willie to come quick, mouthing "hurry up, hurry up."

Willie bolted. A dead sprint across the yard, clothes under one arm, toothbrush in his teeth, boots flapping. He dove into the car, turned the key, and that old engine roared like it had been waiting for its moment.

They peeled out of that gravel patch like hell was on their heels.

"Holy shit!" Willie shouted.

"Holy *shit!*" he said again, laughing now, as if to confirm it was real.

And just like that, they were gone—two lost souls in a rust bucket LeMans, $185 between them, 1989, chasing neon dreams and outrunning all the good sense they didn't have to begin with.

There's something about driving across that punishing stretch of ground between Michigan and the

Mississippi river. It'll break your spirit! It's ugly and brutal. Narrow, boring, flat. Unending strips of plain pavement that make you feel like you're driving on a treadmill. The sky is right on top of you—close enough to suffocate it wears you down. The silence was so dense that the only sounds were the faint rattle of the rear window, the whine of balding tires on blacktop, and the low drone of wind through the gap in the side door. All the while, Willie kept his foot on the gas and his mind on the plan. He knew it'd all be downhill from there if they could just make it to the river and get across. The thought was simple but firm: Once across, there'd be no turning back. The twelve-hour drive would stretch into twenty-one, maybe twenty-two, if his trusty LeMans held together. He was sure they would make it, had to make it. Then all the pressure would be off. Then it was just a long, slow roll into Vegas.

But getting to the big river was no small victory.

Willie knew that. He told me he almost lost it before they made it. It was the merciless bottlenecks between Michigan City and Joliet that really got to him. Logjam after logjam of semis, moving vans and RVs. Pure Hell, he said. It's along that stretch of road that he nearly ditched the whole thing and turned back. He knew that once they hit the river, they'd be "on the other side." At least that's what he called it. He thought the view would change, the clouds would open up, and they'd be free and clear. Of course, the wide-open spaces would bring their own kind of mental circus. But, again, at least they'd be on the other side, he said. Whatever the hell that meant.

"Where are we now?" Lexi asked around mid-day, kicking her feet up on the dash and lighting another cigarette. They'd already burned through the first tank of gas and a six-pack of Hamm's.

"Still Illinois," Willie said.

"You're kidding."

"Told you it was one long bastard."

Lexi shook her head. "It's like we're not moving."

"Tell me about it," he said. "About lost my mind already."

"We'll make it," she said. "We're close to the river, right?"

"Close enough."

But Willie wasn't so sure.

He said it took an eternity to break free of the city sprawl. Then the horizon opened up, but not in the way he imagined.

The wide open skies on the west side of the Mississippi, especially when you reach desert, has a way of making everything feel temporary—like even time itself is just passing through. That's the headspace Willie Lyonsan found himself in as he rattled west across state lines in that beat-to-hell LeMans, a rusted-out chariot carrying a redhead with a busted past and a man freshly married to someone he hadn't said goodbye to.

The plan, if you could call it that, was simple: keep driving until they hit Vegas. No calls. No looking back. Just pavement and sky and a whole lot of bad ideas stitched together with caffeine and bravado. The radio barely worked. It gave them two options: AM gospel and crackling mariachi. Lexi flipped it off and hummed to herself instead— some half-remembered country song, soft as wind.

Willie was quiet. The kind of quiet where you're not thinking about the road but about everything you just left behind and what might be waiting at the next truck stop. He wanted to feel free, but the guilt stuck to him like desert sweat. Hui Ko. Pok. The delivery job he'd flubbed so hard it didn't even qualify as sabotage—it was more like performance art. And his family. His family had no clue what he was up to—not that they'd be all that surprised anyway.

And yet, he laughed. Out of nowhere. Some deep, wild laugh like the kind you let loose when you realize you've gone too far to turn back.

"Christ," he muttered. "What the hell are we doing?"

Lexi just smirked and lit another cigarette.

"Same thing everybody's doing, babe. Running from something."

They'd been driving for hours when the LeMans started to groan—some rattling noise under the hood like a pocketful of loose change in a clothes dryer. The heat warped the highway. Mirage country. Nothing but horizon and heatwaves. That's when they spotted it: a flickering motel sign off the highway, bent and leaning like a drunk old man.

The Starlite - Vacancy.

It looked like it hadn't seen a renovation since Elvis faked his death. A horseshoe of tired little rooms wrapped around a parking lot the color of scorched toast. A single bulb flickered above the office door. Willie parked under it, engine coughing its last breath.

Inside, they found a front desk manned by a tall, half-blind old man in a bolo tie and pressed slacks. He looked like he'd been waiting specifically for *them*.

"No need for a name," he rasped, handing Willie a key.

"Just remember—some doors don't open unless you close the right one first."

Willie blinked and cocked his head. "What?"

But the old man just smiled like he'd dropped a Bible verse and walked away.

Lexi leaned into Willie as they walked to the room.

"Creepy old dudes say creepy shit. Let's take a shower before I lose my damn mind."

Later that night, wrapped in motel sheets still warm from the desert day, Lexi stared at the ceiling, her cigarette tracing lazy smoke rings that the ceiling fan—half working—refused to disturb.

"I tell you I've been married before?" she asked, voice flat.

Willie turned to her. "No. But I'd be more surprised if you hadn't."

She chuckled. "Once, legally, to a guy in the army. Big boots, small brain. Didn't last. The other was a girl named Rina. Bartender in Biloxi. Wild as hell. She left me for a pastor."

Willie didn't say anything.

"I got a kid too," she said after a long pause. "Girl. Three years old. I haven't seen her since she was born."

Now he turned. "Wow, Lex."

"She's with my mom. Which is its own kind of nightmare. I wasn't ready. Still ain't. I'm not headed to Vegas for fun, Will. I'm running from Kentucky. From court dates. From my name."

Willie exhaled slow. The ceiling fan clunked overhead like it was trying to keep time with his heartbeat.

"We're not there yet," he said finally.

"What?"

"Vegas. Life. Any of it. We're not there yet. Let's just... be in the middle for a while."

Lexi reached over and held his hand without looking at him.

They hit the road the next morning, late and sunburnt, vending machine coffee burning their throats. Somewhere near the Utah-Arizona-Nevada line, Willie missed a turn—maybe on purpose—and they ended up in a place that didn't seem to exist on any map.

The town had no name. Just a rusty old sign that said "POSTED." No gas station, no people. Just abandoned buildings holding onto their last bit of shape. The sun lit everything in high contrast—burned-out beauty.

They spotted a dusty old bank building with a wooden stoop and two cracked rocking chairs. Willie parked, killed the engine, and they just sat.

"Think anyone lives here?" Lexi asked.

"Doubt it. Place looks like God quit halfway through."

She pulled out a soda from the cooler—RC Cola, flat but cold—and handed it to him.

"You ever think we're just ghosts from different timelines?" she asked.

"All the time."

She turned to him, eyes soft now. "What do you want, Willie? I mean really. What's the endgame?"

He took a sip, looked out at the empty street, trying to be dramatic.

"I want to land in a place where nobody's waiting on me to be anything but tired," he said.

Lexi nodded like she understood too well. She kissed him—not sexy, not hungry—just human. Like a promise. Or maybe a goodbye.

They pulled out of that ghost town just as the sun began to fold itself into the horizon. The LeMans roared back to life like it had been given a second chance.

In the rearview, the town was already gone— dissolving into dust, memory, maybe myth.

Lexi fell asleep in the passenger seat, her head resting against the door, red hair lit gold by the dying light.

Willie kept driving, hands loose on the wheel, eyes fixed on the straight line ahead.

Vegas shimmered in the distance like a promise Willie had no business believing in. He told me later that somewhere in that moment—sun bleeding out in front of them, Lexi asleep beside him, the engine humming like a lullaby—he could already feel it coming to an end. Not just the drive. The *whole thing.* That wild, beautiful escapade was already folding into memory before it was even over.

This all happened some thirty years ago now. Eight days, he once told me. That's how long he knew Lexi. Eight days. But she still lives in the soft corners of his story—those places reserved for people who mattered more than time allows. They shared something—brief, chaotic, intimate, sacred. A spiritual bond forged in quick getaways, motel sheets, ghost towns, and gas station coffee. No regrets. None that he's ever confessed, anyway.

He never contacted Hui Ko again. Said it wouldn't have been right. His cousin, a paralegal back in Michigan, took care of the paperwork and made sure it all got served proper.

He never heard from Lexi again, either. That part, I think, stung a little. But whenever her name comes up—and it does, usually with a grin and a shake of the head—he smiles. That Willie smile, the one that says *I lived through it* and *I wouldn't change a thing*.

That eight-day detour kept him in the West for almost a decade.

California, Nevada, New Mexico... he got lost in it all. Or maybe it found *him*. Hard to say with Willie. The adventures didn't stop—they just changed their clothes.

But Lexi? Lexi was the spark that lit the fuse.

Scene 4

The Mob Called

Willie's first stint out west, after Lexi took the other fork in the road in Vegas, had him bouncing around Northern Arizona and Utah for several months before finally heading across Nevada and landing in California. Once there it didn't take him long to find the next rabbit hole filled with someone else's unresolved trauma to scurry down. This one took the form of a rather featured, French-African blues singer named Nina Duplessis...eight years his senior.

Willie never had trouble finding work, he had the most intuitive mind I've ever come across. From a young age he could speak with authority on most topics and trades, from house framing to politicking to wrench turning and marketing strategies. He'd earn just enough to stay in whiskey and dry boots. Beyond that? He never thought much about it. Willie was endlessly social. His preference though, oddly, was to be alone with his thoughts. But his heart and his intellect simultaneously yearned to wade in, connect, observe and engage with folks across all social and economic lines. He had a knack for it.

He traded the LeMans for a pick up truck in Elko, Nevada before, remarkably, passing through Reno—I would have lost that bet—and making his way across into California. From there he headed south, sensing his next zip code wasn't far off. And damned if he didn't sniff it out. Like a beagle with a bead on a rabbit he had a compass for finding places not made to be found—where the quietly inspired lamented. This town wasn't on any map worth trusting—somewhere between Julian's old soul and Ramona's dusty underbite. You had to squint to see it, or maybe bleed a little first. It wasn't so much a town as a *pause* in the world, a stretch of road that artists and oddballs passed through and never quite managed to leave. There were wind chimes made from bicycle gears, blown glass lamps hanging from tree limbs, and the low hum of a reel-to-reel echoing through a shack with no address. . He called it "a place that smelled like turpentine and all the mistakes people meant to outgrow but didn't." It was the kind of hideout where ex-musicians worked tables at the diner or welded angels by daylight and by moonlight, cut demo tapes. Naturally, it's where Willie ran across Nina—sultry, brilliant, and about as safe to touch as a copper wire in a thunderstorm.

Nina Duplessis was a long and curvy French woman of West African descent. Her strikingly beautiful skin was so dark it held a luster—like polished obsidian soaking in midnight that caught every room off guard. Nina was the queen of the blues. Semi-famous at one time. She had a singing career that never quite made the turn, though, touring with regional acts up and down the Delta. Even toured with Ike and Tina one summer in Europe as a backup singer. She had the pipes. She had the look. Hell, she had the whole damn package. But her temperament buried her. Regal as a queen and elegant as a cat walking silk, she could command a room just by entering it—until the wrong word, or the wrong man, set her off. More often than not, she had a snifter of Courvoisier in one hand and one of her heels in the other, ready to hurl it at whatever promoter, manager, or poor bastard had crossed her that night. Talent like hers would have sold out rooms from Harlem to Montreux—if only her fire hadn't burned the bridges faster than she could build them.

Her and Willies worlds collided one night at Josies, a little biker bar hidden up in the hills run by a local legend, a fiercely loved pioneering woman in her late 50's, who was usually there behind the bar. Willie ambled in one night, Nina was on the stage belting out her rendition of "I've got to use my imagination", in a much more Bobby Bland flavor than Gladys Knight—slow and gritty with a tempo that grooved through the floor. Only a handful of people sat at the bar. They locked eyes when he walked in. Most men, too intimidated to gaze too long, he couldn't look away. She noticed. He wasn't trying to be cool, he had a genuine fascination with this unexpected brilliant ball of seductive electricity coming from the stage. He smiled. She smiled. The die had been cast.

She finished her set and walked to the bar where Josie had a Manhattan waiting for her. Willie was a handful of barstools down on a bend in the bar where he had a head on view of her. She grabbed a cigarette and her glass, and with a lingering look towards Willie headed towards the back door. Willie grabbed his whiskey and beer and headed in that direction, stopping briefly to grab a book of matches from a tray on the bar.

The back door opened to a wooden patio where staff would break. Nina was leaning on the rail, back to the door, staring out at a small patch of moonlit woods on the other side of a small side lot. Willie slowed his pace a half step to observe the long, green, one-piece, form fitting bodycon dress she was wearing, and wearing well. He walked up beside her and lit a match. She leaned in and touched the end of the cigarette to the flame, and after an easy drag she blew the match out, smoke curling towards the sky. She turned back towards the woods. He leaned over and looked in the same direction. Willie could talk in any situation. I'm sure Nina could too. But silence was the right move right then, a perfect fit, it felt right. Several minutes passed, both still gazing out towards the woods, Willie finally said "good choice on the tempo of My Imagination. Had more of a Bobby Bland vibe to it."

"Noticed that, did you?" she said

"Who wouldn't" he quipped.

She chuckled in amusement.

"Nina"

"Willie"

"Haven't seen you around"

"Just moved to town. Renting a room from a lady they call Miss Patty behind the farmers market.

"I love her", Nina responded, "She's been here longer than anyone. You were a lucky bastard to get a room there."

"She seems like a great person."

"The best. You plan on staying?"

"As far as I know. Only been here a few weeks but it seems like a good fit. My kinda' people."

"Where you from, you don't need to respond."

"Michigan. You? And you *do* need to respond", Willie said with a chuckle.

She laughed, "Mississippi Delta!"

"Huh, would've never guessed", Willie said with a grin.

With an approving grin and a slight shake of the head she said "I need to get back in for my last set. You sticking around?"

"For a bit", he said.

She turned and walked back towards the door. As she was walking away she said, "Thanks for the light, Willie."

"Thanks for the chat, Nina."

Willie stayed at the rail, breathing in the night air and reflecting on the simpleness of the conversation. In fact, he stayed at that rail for the better part of the next hour, finally going in as Nina was finishing her last song. Another handful of people had filtered in. He walked past the stage and angled towards the door. He stopped short and leaned against the bar between two stools and listened to her sing her last note. He applauded with the rest of the crowd, shot her a warm smile and eased his head backwards slightly with a nod, as if to say, I'll see you again, she understood the gesture and returned the same nod with a smile, and out the door he went.

You couldn't chart Willie's path in straight lines. His life never moved that way. It zigged when others zagged, looped when logic begged for a conclusion. So when he ghosted California after a wrecking-ball love affair named Nina Duplessis, no one was surprised. What was surprising, though, was the string of unlikely events that led to the demolition, catapulted him out of town and spun into the most unlikely commission.

It's no surprise Willie had an affinity for the low lit rough edges of, well, just about everything. It is particularly shown through in his photography. He never sought attention. That was half his magic—he just *was*, and people somehow noticed. The same way a desert flower catches your eye not by shouting its colors, but by simply blooming in the middle of nowhere. That's how this whole unlikely saga started.

Unbeknownst to him, one of his old girlfriends back in Beaverton had submitted a handful of his portraits to *Amateur Photography Magazine*. She was enamored with his work. Willie would've hated the gesture in theory, but the magazine apparently loved it. They ran two shots: one of a farmhand with blood on his jeans and sunrise in his eyes, and one of another hand framed perfectly against a backdrop on the same farm, leaning against a splintered corral post. They each looked like two dark desperate souls from the dust bowl era. Minimalist. Raw. Poetic.

Now, enter Frank Rizzo—retired muscle from Cicero, west of Chicago—turned olive oil importer turned patron of the arts. Big on Sinatra, bigger on Marlboros, and for reasons known only to his private musings and his box of vinyl records, *huge* on cowboy lore. Something about the code of the old west made sense to a man who came up with omertà stitched into his DNA.

While waiting for his weekly manicure—I'm serious, the guy had standards—he sees Willie's photos in the magazine and something clicks. The grit, the silence, the reverence for solitude. "This kid gets it," he tells the lady sitting next to him. "I want a book full of these. Real cowboys. Not the ones staged in belt buckles the size of dinner plates. The ghosts who never came in from the range. I gotta find this Willie Lyonsan."

But how do you find a guy like Willie? Even at 23 he'd already made a short career out of *not* being found.

Frank knew publishers around Chicago. He was able to connect a few dots and found out about the girl who submitted the photos. He had his niece call her. She told her the last she'd heard Willie was bouncing around out West near Vegas, or maybe Reno.

"Ya wanna find Willie? Simple", she said, "Find the dive bars on his trail and ask the right bartender. He won't be hard to find."

Willie left traces in the folds of whispered memory. He'd crash in a small town, shoot for a few weeks, charm the locals, buy drinks, trade stories, leave a print behind the bar somewhere, then vanish. And these hideout towns—they talk. Word gets around. So Frank sends a couple feelers— quiet, polite ones—from Reno he knew to do a little diggin' into the smoke-filled corners of seedy cantinas and desert roadhouses in the area. And eventually, someone says, "You lookin' for the drifter with the camera? Might check around Ramona."

They reported this back to Frank. Now, Frank's no dummy. He doesn't send suits. He sends family. Stephanie

Giordano—his niece, half Italian, half velvet hammer. A fixer. Mid-30s, sharp as a tack, and not afraid to throw an elbow in a boardroom or a barroom. She'd grown up around the business but steered clear of the darker corners. Music degree. She was a virtuoso on the violin. Fiercely intelligent. And, crucially, impossible to rattle. Frank sends her with a mission: *"Find the cowboy whisperer and convince him this book isn't a hustle."*

She rolls into town in a beat-up Jeep with Illinois plates and finds him, of course. Sitting alone in the corner of the bar, sipping bourbon, camera bag slumped like a tired saddle next to him. It takes about three minutes for Willie to realize she's not local. Five minutes to figure out she's not like the others. And ten minutes to realize he's in trouble again. But this time, it ain't a woman with eyes full of secrets. It's a mob niece with a publishing budget.

"You're Willie Lyonsan, right?" she said, not asking.

Willie looked up from his glass, gave her the kind of once-over you save for someone who could either hire you or have you buried in the desert. "Depends. Who's asking?"

She pulled up a stool beside him without waiting for an invite. "Stephanie Giordano. My uncle Frank—he's a big admirer. Saw some of your work in *Amateur Photographer* a few months back. You shot a black-and-white of a couple farmhands in Michigan?"

Willie furrowed his brow. "I'm not published anywhere. Must be someone else's work."

"Nope, it's you. Your ex submitted the photos to the magazine. Julia, I think. Or Julie."

Willie groaned, rubbed the bridge of his nose. "Jesus."

Stephanie smiled. "Relax. It was good. Real good. Enough for Frank to send me cross-country to find you and make an offer."

She reached into her satchel and slid a weathered manila envelope down the bar. Inside was a rough proposal. Title page read: *Cowboys of the West – A Portrait Series.*

"Frank wants a book. Big one. Real cowboys. No actors, no Rodeo riders. He's footing the bill—travel, film, development. You shoot, we handle the rest."

Willie thumbed through the pages. His jaw tensed.

"Not interested in some glorified mafia-funded coffee table vanity project."

Stephanie shrugged. "Then don't make it that. Make it yours. Frank's just the bankroll. You're the eye."

He didn't say anything right away. Just looked out the dusty window toward a horizon nobody had drawn yet. He'd been drifting, aimless. This... this was a direction. Even if it was built on mob money and ex-girlfriend submissions.

"I'll think about it," he muttered.

"Good," she said, standing. Then, almost as an afterthought: "Oh, and I'm staying in town. Don't worry, not with you. I'll be around. Helping out. Fixing things."

Willie looked back at her. "You're what now?"

She grinned. "I'm your assistant, Willie. Didn't I mention that?"

He stared at her a long beat. Then laughed. Not because it was funny, but because fate always had a flair for theater with him.

They spent the next few weeks together, based out of Santa Ysabel, bouncing between ranches, gathering stories, dodging trouble. He was shooting. She was fixing. Nina? Nina was watching from the shadows. When he could carve out the time, he'd do his best to make Nina happy. Dinners. Hanging out in town. Overnights. He'd go see her sing at Josies. But there was a slow boil brewing from underneath. No one—not even Willie—saw how far this was going to spiral.

Day excursions with Stephanie turned into overnights. They'd be gone chasing ghosts and shadows for days at a time. Treks would take them all the way to the borderlands, through wild-eyed ranches, outlaw country, and stories so tangled they'd leave scars. But for now, it started with a drink, a folder, and a girl who didn't ask—she just stayed.

Willie started to fall for her. Not in the way he fell for Lexi or the others. This wasn't hearts and flowers. It was respect. Mutual fire. A grudging admiration that turned, quietly, into something else. And he was laser focused on the mission of finding cowboys. He loved it. It suited him perfectly. I remember him calling me and telling me about it one night: "Oscar, these cowboys... they don't want to be found, they're ghosts. Living fossils. And they're vanishing, man. Nobody's telling their story. I feel like I was built for this project."

I saw some of the proofs once. Jesus. They weren't portraits, they were monuments. Lines on faces like dry riverbeds. Eyes that'd seen too much and said nothing. It was his finest work. And, unsurprisingly, it almost got him killed.

The next few weeks looked like the previous few—he and Stephanie bouncing between ranches, gathering stories, dodging trouble. There was this one trip, down by the border, where the cattle trails meet the no-man's-land between Arizona and Sonora. Willie had heard about a rancher who ran his cattle close to cartel territory. Figured he'd make for a compelling subject. And he was right. But what he didn't know—what he couldn't have known—was that the rancher had just found a body. Or part of one.

Willie and Stephanie showed up just as the Federales were hauling it away.

He looked over at Stephanie and said, "you see that guy? He had no face. It was just...gone."

Stephanie didn't respond, just nodded.

Through sheer curiosity, and maybe a little adrenaline from the scene that had just unfolded before them, they stuck around anyway—holed up in an old bunkhouse. Stephanie—every bit as daring as Willie, maybe more so—seemed to forget they'd come to this barren border town to photograph a cowboy for Frank's book. Instead, she got it in her head to detour from the mission and chase something more interesting. Something worth framing. Didn't take much to convince Willie.

They'd been staking out the edge of town near the feed depot, hoping to catch a glimpse of the rougher traffic that was said to roll through after dusk—coyotes, smugglers, cartel lookouts in civilian clothes. Willie had posted up on a crate near the corrugated fence line, camera poised just above the slats. Stephanie was tucked behind the old livestock scales with a flask of something that leeched a strong, diesel like odor into the dead air around them.

That's when the headlights came—slow, deliberate, like someone wasn't in a rush to be anywhere they were supposed to be. Willie steadied his lens and pulled focus. The truck coasted by once, turned around at the edge of the arroyo, and rolled back even slower, this time stopping just short of where the fence jutted out toward the main road. The window dropped. Nothing said. Just a long, cold stare from the driver's side—a man, the moon lighting his cheekbones like blades sat with one wrist curled around the steering wheel with the other resting just out of view.

Willie, itching to take the once in a lifetime shot eased himself up slowly, just a few inches more.

"Don't," Stephanie hissed, barely audible. "Wait!"

But it was too late. Willie squeezed off a shot—just one. The shutter snapped like a firecracker in the silence.

The truck's reverse lights blinked, and the engine gunned in a tight arc. The back tires kicked up a spray of gravel as it lunged toward the fence line. Willie darted back, tripping over a feed bucket, scrambling for the bunkhouse.

They didn't make it.

The front door splintered on the first hit, the frame cracking like a wishbone. Two men—one wiry, one wide—

stormed in, guns low. Not amateurs. Not local. Stephanie grabbed the camera, threw it behind the mattress and shoved Willie hard, out the broken side window and into the brush. They ran like hell was on their heels—it probably was. No flashlight. Just blind panic and the sound of boots thudding like horses galloping behind them, snapping mesquite and curses in Spanish.

They outran them and hid in a culvert all night, tangled in brush, shivering in silence while the desert buzzed and sighed above them. Stephanie kept her arm across Willie's chest like a seatbelt, as if sheer will could hold him in place.

That might've been the end of them both, if it weren't for Stephanie.

At first light they made their way back to town, got in the Jeep and headed back to Cali.

Now for reasons known only to whatever gods kept throwing matches at Willie's gasoline-soaked life, the timing of the two of them rolling back into Santa Ysabel could not have been worse. With Willie behind the wheel of Stephanie's Jeep, and the two of them snuggled up pretty close in laughter, Nina drove by. Seeing them together like that proved too much. As she wheeled around, tires screeching, eyes narrowed, she gave chase. Pure instinct took over and Willie bolted like a rabbit.

"What are you running for?" Stephanie exclaimed.

"You don't know Nina"

"I know her type, pull over, I'll set her straight!"

Just then a police cruiser happened by, whipped around and gained quickly.

"Thank God", Willie breathed in relief.

The chase ended how you'd expect: flashing lights, two squad cars now, one shattered rear view mirror. Nina screaming as they cuffed her. Willie dazed, heart pounding. Stephanie, calm as ever, typing away on her phone.

Willie told me later, "Oscar, that woman turned into a banshee with a V8."

He and Stephanie drove back to town, pulled into the tavern, ordered a couple whiskey's and sat in silence recounting the last few days.

"I think we have enough for the book", Stephanie said.

"Agreed."

"Think I'll head back in the morning."

"It's been a hell of a run these last six weeks", Willie said, looking down at his glass.

"I'll never forget it", Stephanie said in a softer tone.

The two of them had grown pretty close. I think she meant a lot to Willie. This was a girl who matched his intellect, and wasn't afraid of living all in, like no one he'd met.

They spent the night at her place and when Willie woke up, she was gone.

He walked the quarter mile back to Miss Patty's, told her he was leaving and headed east, sun in his eyes, with the few things he rolled into town with and the itch of something unfinished in his bones. The desert was getting into his spirit. Fit him like a glove. Arizona took him in like a stray dog with a busted paw. And for a while, he let it. The wind was warm, the desert wide, and the light—good God, the light—it carved everything into something worth remembering.

He crossed over at Blythe and meandered around for a few days. Headed north to Parker. Back down to Salome. He made his way into Wickenburg, where he almost stayed, but felt the urge to press east further. He spotted a 'For Rent' sign in front of a tattered iron gate that blocked a short driveway that led maybe 50 yards back to a dilapidated, flat roofed, cobbled together shack of a house with a big porch jutting out the side. It was up the hill just on the edge of what looked to be Main Street in Cave Creek. An old timer was locking up the place and headed towards the gate.

"Interested, young fella'?"

"I am. I'll take it", he said.

"Ya haven't seen it and don't know how much I'm asking."

"Don't need to and don't care. I'll be on that porch most of the time."

"I love that porch", the old man said. "Sat there 50 years."

"$400 a month."

Willie reached into his pocket and pulled out 8 100 dollar bills.

"Here's first and last."

"Ok then. I'll drop the lease off later. Try to keep the Javelina out from under the house. If you need to turn off the water, here's the tool and here's the hole. There's a couch in there, not much else. You got any furniture?"

"Nah, I'll make do."

The old man handed him a key. "Welcome home..."

The old man passed through the gate, walked to his truck, and drove off.

Willie went inside to find a halfway decent sized living room, wood floors throughout, a small kitchen to the left, a short hallway straight ahead with a small bedroom to the right and a small bathroom to the left. The walls were bare, plumbing barely-plumb, and he could hear the drone of a swamp cooler that sounded like a failing freight train humming above. But that porch. From that porch you could see the desert pull itself over the earth like a faded quilt. Willie sat out there most nights, drinking something brown, fiddling with old lenses, and sketching out ideas to find the next ghost.

For the better part of the next three years, Willie uncharacteristically kept to himself. He loved everything about this dusty old cowboy town. Felt right at home. Was in sync with the energy of it from the moment he landed, but he was in a different headspace. He'd wander down the hill into town to listen to the band and grab a beer but didn't engage much with anyone. Between Lexi, Nina and the harrowing project with Stephanie I think he'd spent a lot of his emotional cache in the years before he rolled into Cave Creek.

Three years was longer than he'd spent anywhere outside of Beaverton. But if you know Willie like I do, you would know that stillness doesn't suit him for long. And though Cave Creek had been a kind of balm, a place where the dust finally settled and the nights felt honest, he still hadn't put all the ghosts to bed. Not by a long shot.

He made a couple off-hand remarks to his landlord about winding up his stay. They'd forged quite a friendship, sipping whiskey together, telling stories. Willie genuinely liked the old guy and he liked Willie. Out on the porch, they had an exchange one night.

"Tom, I'm thinking about wrapping it up and moving on."

"Hate to see you go."

"Been thinking about getting one of those old travel trailers, small enough for my pick up, and roam around a little."

"Did that myself a number of years back. It's a good life."

"Tell ya what", Tom eluded, "if you end up getting that RV, and ever want to come back this way, I'll put you a hook up right there on that lot next door. Be a perfect spot for you."

"No kidding! Thanks, Tom. I may just take you up on that."

One day, about a week later, without much fanfare—with a short and half-drunk bottle of Dickel left on the porch—Willie was gone. No destination shared, no story offered.

Just gone. I didn't hear from him for about a year. He eventually made his way back to Beaverton.

He called it his sabbatical later. Said he needed to find out if the rest of the world could still surprise him. Said there were still some debts to pay, favors to return, wounds to bury in places that had never heard his name.

What he didn't say, but what I've come to believe, is that he was looking for proof he could still feel something. Anything.

Arizona had steadied him. But steadiness ain't the same as healing. And Willie Lyonsan... well, he's never been one to settle for just getting *almost* anywhere.

Oh, Christ! Almost forgot. This is as good a place as any to tell you about Lou. Good ol' Lou...

Scene 5

The Maria Incident

Willie drifted slowly back toward Beaverton after leaving Arizona. And when I say slow, I mean molasses-in-January slow. He spent the better part of a year meandering West to East, South to North—like deer prints through a stand of pines after a fresh Michigan snow. Wandering aimlessly, but somehow with purpose. True to form, he'd blow into some forgotten burg, pick up part-time work and a cot in the back of a gas station, charm the locals like they were old friends just waiting to be reintroduced, shoot a few rolls of film, maybe fall into a woman's good graces—and then slide out again, quiet as smoke, like a note on the breeze.

After a long and winding circle through the American landscape, Willie finally found himself back in Beaverton, that little haven of familiarity tucked away like a worn book under a pile of glossy new magazines. No sooner than he dusted off the Michigan snow he confessed his true sentiments.

Practically the minute he touched the doorknob he said, "Oscar, the West is where my heart beats the loudest. Skies here are too damn low," as though the Midwest had a permanent ceiling that kept him from taking deep enough breaths. "The roads are too narrow."

It was like he had to stoop his shoulders and tuck in his elbows just to exist back home now. Willie told me he wanted to spend time with the family and all of us, but he was already scheming his way back to Arizona. The plan was half-baked and vague—just the way he liked it—but it was alive between his ears.

"Let's get on the bike and head over to Krzysiak's" Willie barked one day.

"Krzysiak's! It's 40 degrees out, and Krzysiak's is 40 minutes from here. Let's take the truck.

"Ok, pussy", he laughed.

Krzysiak's is arguably the best Polish restaurant on earth, including anywhere in Poland. The Kielbasa will curl your toes and the Pierogi, my God the Pierogi.

We made our way over, ate til we burst, stopped and had a couple PBR's at some tiny, neighborhood tavern— according to local lore there are somewhere around 600 bars in Bay City, Michigan—and then headed back towards Beaverton.

Willie decided to go up along Saginaw Bay and then cut over to Gladwin and drop down from there, which was odd. We never went this way. Guess it was all that wandering he did, just decided to take a wider loop.

As we rolled through White Star, about half way to Gladwin, we passed a small block building, an animal rescue, with a sign out front that read Adopt-a-Pet Today. Willie slowed down, pulled a three point turn in somebody's driveway and pulled into the lot.

"You adopting a pet today, Willie."

"Maybe. Wanna take a look."

The lot was empty with the exception of a lone dusty Buick LaSabre. When we walked in, the front desk was unmanned. We looked around, waited for a couple minutes —not Willie's strong suit—and Willie went for the door handle. You could hear dogs barking on the other side of it. There was a sign on it that said 'Staff Only'.

"To hell with it, I'm going in."

We went in and Willie tracked straight to the back of the building like a laser—hardly glancing at any of the dogs, like following a voice he heard in his head. He was a couple steps ahead of me. He turned the corner almost at the rear exit and as I rounded the corner he was crouched down with his fingers protruding through the chain link gate of the very last kennel. The dog inside, an oversized Boston, was sitting regal as a lion at the rear corner of the kennel, half looking at us and half uninterested.

Willie said, "I want him. He speaks to me. I know him from somewhere."

The name on the card outside the kennel read, LeBaron.

By this time a very irritated young lady came around the corner and said, "you two are *NOT* supposed to be back here. Please go back up front in the waiting area."

Willie replied, "I'm sorry, Miss, I just came to get my dog, LeBaron."

"LeBaron is *your* dog?"

"Yep", Willie replied. "Well, he is now. I want him. We had a talk and he's agreed to come home with me."

With a somewhat annoyed chuckle she said, "come on up front, I'll bring him up."

$85 bucks and a few signatures later, we were headed home. Willie, LeBaron and me. Three abreast in the pickup. He wasn't scared or shook up at all. It was like just another Tuesday to this dog. He had a look on his face as if to say, "Where we going? Meh! It doesn't matter." It was the damndest thing.

"LeBaron", Willie said. "That is a stupid name."

I swear that dog looked at Willie in agreement.

"Lou. You're definitely Lou."

Again, looked over, like he agreed! I watched them pull a fascinating focus on each other almost instantly. From that day on, Willie and Lou were a unit.

Willie changed that day. Not for the better, not for the worse, just changed. He had a different focus that seemed to curb his restlessness, *some*. It didn't remove it, if anything he was more determined to seek out new adventure, but with his new costar. Maybe he became more of a magnet for it. His force in the universe was double dose now.

Yep, from the day they found each other you couldn't say "Willie" without "Louie" shadowing close behind—like an echo with a soul. Anyone who spent more than a minute around Lou forgot he was a dog at all. He was no ordinary dog. That's for sure. Not even close.

Not your Westminister variety Boston Bull, Lou was thicker-set and blocky. His forty pounds pressed the outer limits of his breed's blueprint. But he carried that heft like a bluesman carries heartbreak—with swagger and grace. His eyes were steady and deep, like a night watchman's lantern, and behind them you saw something more than instinct— you saw memory.

When they set eyes on each other it was like it had been written. It wasn't just love at first sight—it was something deeper. An agreement, maybe. A silent contract forged in the soft space between two misfits who had no business being caged.

They moved through life like a reconnaissance team. Quiet. Calculated. Always together. Willie never trained Louie in any traditional sense because he never had to. Willie said they'd had a few 'discussions' early on but Lou seemed to know what Willie was after. Second discussions were never required. They were on the same frequency. Together they moved through crowds, alleys, parades, and dive bars with the precision of Navy SEALs and the calm of a couple monks—never a leash, never a collar. He didn't own either.

Willie rigged a custom seat on the Kawasaki, where the front of the seat met the rear of the tank—a Frankenstein blend of fiberglass, surplus canvas, and duct tape ingenuity —where Lou would perch, goggles strapped over his eyes and a neck scarf snapping behind him like a battle-flag of freedom. They looked like some cinematic fever dream. Willie at the helm, grin set in place; Louie just ahead of him, unmoved by speed, wind, or stares. It was something to see.

They were a viral spectacle on that vintage steed. Every ride turned heads: windows would roll down, phones would come out, and someone always shouted, "I love your dog!"

Louie didn't just ride shotgun—he *was* the shotgun. He was Willie's compass. His wingman. His conscience. His stillness. On first dates, Lou came along. On whiskey runs, Lou came along. Through the years, through the laughter, heartbreak, and hangovers, Lou was there—an ever-present reminder that loyalty doesn't bark or beg. It just *is*.

They were welded together. Man and dog. Not as pet and owner, but as brothers in arms. Co-conspirators. Living proof that sometimes, if you're lucky, you find the one soul on this earth who already understands you—no training required.

Which brings us to the bars. *You knew we'd get there...*

Willie and Lou made stories for folks far and wide in all four directions. Like a beacon in the sky, wherever they lived or roamed, they tracked to the gritty, out of the way bars where only locals went. Without fail, they were always welcomed in like returning family. The rhythm of this peculiar united front was ever present and undeniable.

Beaverton had two such establishments, both emblazoned at the entrance with laminated "No Dogs Allowed" signs posted like commandments. But Louie was the exception. Same was true in a handful of other taverns dotting across America. In each of these he had *his* own stool —an unwritten codex enforced by barkeeps and regulars alike. Locals knew. Adding to their nightly entertainment, they loved the spectacle. But an outsider attempting to slide onto that cushion? The barkeep would smile, point to a naked stool down the bar, and say, "That one's free. This one's Louie's." No irony. Just fact.

In they'd walk, like a choreographed scene. Willie, all swagger and soft eyes, glad-handing his way through the regulars like a mayor in denim. And just a few steps ahead now, Lou—silent, deliberate—moving with the kind of confidence that didn't require fanfare. He'd break off, nose pointed straight at his destination, weaving through stools and boots with the breath of an old sage who'd done this all before. No leash. No nod. No need.

By the time Willie made it halfway to the bar, Lou would already be there, at his stool like it was part of the floor plan. He'd pause for a beat, then hop up with a surprising ease for a dog built like a sack of cannonballs. Once settled, he'd square his haunches and scan the room with the quiet composure of someone who'd seen it all and wasn't terribly impressed. Not in a snide way—Lou wasn't snide. Just seasoned. Like an old jazz man eyeing the band, waiting to see if they could really swing.

A few nods came his way—"Evenin', Louie"—as if he were just another old boy at the bar. And maybe he was. He gave no reply, of course. Just a slow blink of disinterest.

If he felt like wandering, he'd slip down from his stool like a shadow peeling off the wall—silent, fluid, entirely on his own terms. He moved like he belonged to the space, not the people in it. Never disruptive, never needy, and never once glancing back to see if Willie was watching. There was no need. Their trust was bone-deep. They always knew where the other one was without ever stopping to look. Their bond felt ancient, like something borne by the gods.

He'd pad through the place like he was inspecting it—not for security, but for rhythm. A soft sniff here at the corner of a boot. A slow pause there beside a regular with another story leaking out of him. Maybe he'd scoop up a few scattered pretzels off the floor, delicately, like hors d'oeuvres at a garden party. Maybe he'd allow a stranger to reach out and run fingers through his brindled coat, offering no more acknowledgment than a blink or a lean-in so slight it felt like permission.

And then, when his internal compass decided the loop was complete, he'd glide back through the maze of legs and lost conversations to his stool, hop up with his usual grace, and sit—chin lifted, eyes half-lidded, the picture of a monarch content with the state of his realm. No ceremony. Just Lou, as he was, as he always had been.

Lou never barked. Not once. Willie told me he never heard him utter a sound. His silence wasn't absence—it was presence. He had nothing to prove.

And honestly, what would he even say, if he could? "You're welcome," maybe. Then he'd man-nod once, like he'd just handed you the best advice of your life, and hop back up on his stool without an ounce of fanfare.

Good ol' Lou. Seen Willie through a lot. With Lou, Willie seemed truly ready to make his way back out west and see what was waiting for him up ahead.

Another few years puffed past and he was busting at the seams, his restlessness a tangible thing that followed him around like a weight that was growing heavier with each passing day. He was as restless as I ever saw him.

He called Tom, his Landlord from years before. They took on like only a month had passed. Willie asked him if his offer still stood for the RV lot. It did. Willie told him he'd be back in a few months. Tom said he'd be ready for him. And with that, Willie had a mission and a destination. He and Lou would head West, take their time, and look for an old travel trailer along the way that they could call home. Willie's folks, his sister and a bunch of his friends sent him off proper with quite a shindig. It started in town, at the Hideaway, and ended in his brother-in-law's barn out near the family farm. What a send off. The next morning, I stopped by and helped him load the old Kawasaki parked at his sisters into the back of the truck. Like a scene out of a movie he and Louie waved and off they went.

Barely an hour into the trip he was driving through Niles when he spotted a vintage looking travel trailer for sale alongside an old country road. It was a beautiful farm house with manicured lawns and big red barns. Looked like a Rockwell painting. He knocked on the door and a young guy answered.

"You here about the RV?"

"Yep, looks like a nice one."

As they walked out to the big side yard where it was parked the guy told him it was his grandparents. Age had prevented them from camping for a number of years now. It had just been sitting in the barn. They bought it new in 1996. Looked like it was still new. At just 24 feet, Willie's old truck could pull it without any trouble.

"How much ya asking for it?"

"$2,500. Comes with the hitch and the stabilizer bars, too."

"I'll take it", Willie said, pulling the cash he'd drawn from the bank before he left from an envelope in his pocket. He counted out 25 one hundred dollar bills and handed them to him. The guy already had a signed title ready— probably knowing the first lucky soul who pulled up would take it at that price. He handed it to Willie, helped him back in and hook up, and down the road they went.

"It's home, Lou. Wherever we go, we're home." Lou looked at Willie and then back to the road.

The rest of that trip was as memorable as any they'd taken together before or since. For the next several months they lived hither and yon across the west—about ten towns in total, I guess. Rolling Stone Minnesota. Spearfish South Dakota. Sundance Wyoming. Oshkosh and Lewellen Nebraska. Snyder Colorado. They caught the eclipse. Stayed with a traveling nurse and her little Shih Tzu, Daisy. Explored endless trails through the wetlands and across the plains. They dropped into Boulder through Longmont and made their way up and over the Rockies to Rifle, then Grand Junction. They settled in Moab for a few weeks before meandering down to Williams, West of Flagstaff for a stint, and finally, they landed back in Cave Creek.

With a heads up a few hours out, Tom was there to greet them. He'd cobbled together a 30 amp plug-in, a septic hookup and a water spigot. Even elevated and flattened a nice spot to park the RV.

"She's a beauty, Willie. You did good. You must be Louie!" Tom said. With a slight wag of the tail, Lou approved.

"Got lucky, really. Feels like home inside."

Tom helped him back in, level up and hook up.

Will and Lou were home. There wasn't a twig between that spot and Black Mountain, either—it loomed like a sentinel right out the door. With the awning out, a large patch of plastic lawn rolled out, Willie in an old Adirondack chair he drug over from a pile of dying lawn items, along with a small wooden table with a glass of Buffalo Trace leaving a moistened ring underneath it...this was about as close to heaven as a man could get.

Most of the cobwebs from life leading to this point had been shaken out of Willie's head. He'd been in 'The Creek' for a while now. He settled right into RV living with all the other outlaws, artists, drifters and misfits in town. It didn't take him long to make his mark and claim his territory. He plugged into the Cave Creek scene like it was made for him. He knew every dive bar and bartender from Scottsdale north, and they knew him, and Louie. He had his truck. He had his beloved bike. He had the other half of his soul—who's custom seat was strapped on and always ready for the ride. They were a couple of men about town, making quite a reputation for themselves. Things were going well. Felt like the shoe was about to drop.

And boy did it...

It was a Monday when Willie declared, "Let's go down to Scottsdale and see Bruce at the Green Top, Lou." Bruce— the bartender with stone white hair and a perpetual scowl— loved Willie despite himself. I met him when I came out to visit. Hell of a nice guy. He'd sneak Lou a shot of beer, complain about our timing as we usually strolled in about closing time, then join in the laughter. That night, though, the Green Top was closed. "Forgot it was Monday, Lou," Willie said. "C'mon, we'll try Earl's."

Earl's Tavern sat a block away, on the other side of a big grassy park area. A squat building with a sticky back patio and a sliding glass door that often stuck unless you jiggled it just so. Willie reached for that door—and then it slid open from the inside, as if by sorcery.

And there she stood. Maria Consuelo Ramos.

Willie froze. They were almost nose-to-nose—close enough he caught the sweet trace of jasmine in her hair, clinging to the dry night air. Her hair was a dark waterfall of curls; her big dark eyes were bright and curious; her smile radiant enough to bake s'mores by. In that moment, Willie's world tilted.

Maria was in town for the warm-growing season, part of a familial agricultural education program—pecan orchards were her legacy back in Mexico. Willie, usually quick with a line, froze like he'd been asked to recite Shakespeare on the spot.

"This is Lou," he eventually muttered, motioning to his sober, four-legged friend.

Maria knelt down, stroked Lou behind the ears, and murmured "Hola, Lou." Lou leaned in—a gentleman applauding a queen.

That tiny gesture shattered the ice. Willie, suddenly emboldened, and after a bit of small talk, asked for her number. Not suave. Earnest. She gave it with a smile and a promise to meet "sometime this week." With social cliffhangers, that was as binding as a trust fall.

On Thursday, Willie called her. She answered with a warm accent that made his heart trip. They agreed on Patty's, a local dive bar known for greasy cheeseburgers and a jukebox that swapped outlaw country for '80s rock.

They arrived early—Willie, perpetually punctual, and Lou, forever ready. Maria pulled up in a ride-share—something Willie noted in the back of his head. She wore jeans and a sunset-colored blouse; in that simple outfit she looked effortlessly radiant.

Inside, Skip the bartender called, "Hammy Dickel?" a moniker Willie learned many a bartender when referring to his beloved Hamm's and a Dickel. Willie nodded. "And a Chardonnay" Maria added, surprising everyone including Skip. Chardonnay at Earl's? Unthinkable. He smirked, dusted off a bottle he was surprised they had and poured it anyway, watching as they settled in a quiet booth.

Conversation flowed: her childhood among Mexican pecan groves, the beauty of Arizona monsoons, his endless motorized escapades, Lou's silent philosophy. Laughter punctuated the air; the jukebox eventually roared to life.

When Maria's third glass appeared, Willie noticed the chaperone at the end of the bar that Maria had no intention of disclosing—a woman, alone, in heels, not of Earl's usual clientele.

Willie excused himself, sidled up, and whispered, "How am I doing so far?" They shared a grin.

Maria's friend hopped down, playfully ribbed a red-faced Maria for a "poor choice," and joined her at their table. When Willie came back Maria and her friend Ana were sitting and laughing together at the table.

"How'd you know?" Maria asked.

"You have to get up pretty early in the morning to get one over on me, Maria," Willie quipped.

She had finished her glass and ordered a fourth while he was in the restroom.

Red flags waved. Willie was too infatuated to heed them.

Weeks passed in a delirium of sunlit breakfasts, long afternoon drives, and midnight movies with Lou's makeshift dog-bed at Willie's feet. Maria had the kind of infectious laugh that lit up diners. She had a love for life, animals, music, and slow, intense conversations. A genuinely sweet soul, by any measure.

Against my skeptical forecast, I found myself hoping this wouldn't implode. Three weeks in, came the crack.

They stumbled out of a waterfront bar near the golf course, where neon lights bled into the quiet night, casting eerie shadows over the nearly deserted parking lot. Willie's truck roared to life as they hit the road, aiming for home. But just before they reached their destination, she erupted. It was as if a switch flipped inside her, plunging her into a darkness Willie had never seen. Her eyes blazed with a wild intensity, and she came apart at the seams. Unhinged and volatile, she hurled a torrent of accusations at Willie, calling him every vile name imaginable, charging him with misdeeds so outlandish, so impossible, they seemed crafted from madness itself. Her fury raged on unchecked for a relentless 15 minutes, until she finally punched herself out, collapsing into a stupor right there, slumped over in the passenger seat.

Willie, feeling as if he had just witnessed a live exorcism, left her to sleep in the truck and stumbled inside to his bed, his mind reeling. He lay there, staring at the ceiling, unable to find peace or rest. The events of the night played on a loop in his mind, making sleep almost impossible. The following morning, she appeared in the kitchen, her face serene and refreshed as if she had just enjoyed the most restful slumber of her life. She showered Willie with gratitude for allowing her to sleep in the truck and cheerfully inquired about his breakfast preferences, her demeanor suggesting that the previous night's episode was nothing more than a forgotten dream.

Perplexed, Willie cautiously asked, "Do you remember last night, all the things you said?" Her eyes widened with concern, and she replied, "Oh my God, Willie, did I say anything mean to you?"

As Willie recounted the strange events, her expression shifted from confusion to distress, tears welling up in her eyes and spilling down her cheeks.

"I am so sorry," she stammered, her voice trembling. "I have no memory of saying any of those things... I will gather my things and leave. You don't need this. You don't need to deal with my issues."

True to his nature, Willie's heart softened instantly, and he slipped into his familiar role of nurturer, healer, and solver of problems.

"It's ok, don't cry. Everything will be ok..." he reassured her, his voice gentle and soothing, promising that everything would indeed be alright.

Willie had always possessed an unshakable confidence in his ability to tackle any problem that came his way. Later, in a moment of quiet reflection, he discreetly picked up the phone and called her mother, seeking her seasoned wisdom. Her voice was tinged with concern as she cautioned him, "You don't want any part of this. We've been struggling with it for 30 years. She's the most wonderful person in the world, but she's a chronic alcoholic and she needs serious professional help. You can't help her."

To Willie, these words were not a deterrent but rather a challenge—a call to action. In his mind, it was an invitation to roll up his sleeves and find a solution. With determination burning bright, he resolved to tackle this issue head-on, not just for her, but for her entire family.

Willie had never been exposed to real alcoholism before. Neither of us had, really. Ya there were a few out of control drunks in town all the time, but they weren't part of our everyday lives. We had never seen real, full blown alcoholism up close before. I don't think Willie even believed it existed. Willie is a dreamer. And while he has plenty of problems, he never sees them as problems. He's a Pollyanna, to his core. So his girlfriend has a little drinking problem, no big deal. He'll fix it. With a little love, a few hugs, some counseling sessions with Louie - she'll be fine. Good as new.

He had no idea what he was in for.

Astonishingly, and against all odds, Willie remained by Maria's side for almost five more years. Unwaveringly loyal. He adamantly refused to abandon her. And those years were a relentless repeat of that fateful night just three weeks into their relationship. The situation spiraled into chaos. She lashed out at Willie physically, not just once, but repeatedly. She hurled objects at him, shattered belongings. She struck him. She accused him of every conceivable transgression. She unleashed a torrent of verbal abuse, branding him with every vile name imaginable. Each outburst was claimed to be a blackout, erased from her memory by the next day, leaving Willie trapped in the relentless storm of her fury.

Willie was torn, believing with every fiber of his being that she didn't remember anything. Things had deteriorated severely. Yet, amidst the chaos, there were fleeting moments of connection and normalcy that fueled his hope. He kept reminding himself that she didn't choose this disease. Between the episodes of terror and destruction, she was tender, sincere and vulnerable. That, Willie insisted, was the real Maria. It was enough to keep him in the fight, even if he sometimes doubted whether it was worth it. He knew she would fall but believed she'd rise again and push forward. He thought that as long as she kept fighting, he would too. I think he genuinely loved her. Still does. Deeply. Though, he struggled with the weight of it. He believed Maria was the one for him, even if it felt like an impossible battle. He was determined to slay the beast within her and give her the happy, peaceful life she craved, even if he wasn't sure he was up to the task.

The entire situation was a tangled mess, and I could see how it shattered Willie on so many levels. Emotionally, he was drained. Spiritually, he seemed adrift. Financially, he was nearly bankrupt. Mentally, he was running on fumes. He poured almost every penny he had into trying to solve an unsolvable problem, often in ways that backfired. Part of him knew he was enabling her, yet he couldn't stop himself, like he was pouring gasoline on an already raging fire.

And to make an impossible situation worse, amid all this dark turmoil, the unthinkable happened. He tragically lost his beloved Louie to brain cancer—his anchor, his confidant. He watched Louie deteriorate into a shell of his former self. It didn't take long. Willie would never let him suffer long. Lou started having seizures, long ones. Fifteen, twenty minutes. When it started happening daily, Willie told him, "Louie, if you do this tomorrow we're going to have to bring in help. Please don't make me do it, Lou." Four or five more tomorrows came with the same, devastating seizures. He made the call. Doc Schneider would come out the next morning. Willie and Lou slept that night as they had every night for almost 12 years. Lou inching Willie off most of the pillow and over to the very edge of the bed. It was a long night. They both knew. The next morning the doc showed up, visually shaken. He'd been with Lou for nearly a decade himself. Out on the rolled up turf in front of the RV, under the watchful presence of a now distorted Black Mountain, Lou laid in Willie's lap and drifted off without a sound. Willie was torn apart, shredded, lost in a sea of grief and confusion.

The last couple of years he was connected to Maria, none of us recognized him. Not even his parents. Between losing Louie and the draining battle with Maria's disease, he didn't speak with the same voice. He didn't live with the same vigor. He didn't believe in any of it any more. He became withdrawn. And he started drinking heavily. No longer for the *cheers*. To forget. He gained weight. He looked like hell. I know to this very day he carries a lot of guilt around knowing he failed to solve Maria's problems. He feels like he let her down. I tried to tell him it wasn't his problem to solve. We've all told him. I think he went too far down the rabbit hole.

Towards the end of what I refer to as 'the Maria incident', about a year beyond Lou's departure, I went to see him, still genuinely concerned for what some of us feared might come next. We met up at a quiet tavern on the edge of town. I walked in, he was already sitting there with a Hamm's. And in that moment I saw what could pass as the faintest glimmer of light back in his eyes, thankfully. Like he might have seen a spot in the distance, beyond the rubble to focus on. The conversation and his tone revealed he was still shaken, and still nowhere near himself. But I could also see he'd found a switch inside, like he was finally looking for a way back to Willie. A handful of beers in, towards the end of our conversation, he told me he was going to take the last of his money and spend a month in Japan, that he'd figure out what was next while he was there.

Willie converted to Buddhism when he was about 25. He has an affinity for the practice. It resonates with him. The temple he joined is in downtown Denver. He'd found it when he lived in Golden and he's stayed close to the Sangha ever since.

The Reverend was a Sensei who had been recruited away from the mother temple in Kyoto. He was immediately captivated by Willie, sensing a unique spirit within him. Together, they forged a profound and enduring friendship. In a gesture of deep respect and connection, the Sensei bestowed upon Willie a Dharma name, 'Shaku Goho,' a name that perfectly encapsulated his role, meaning 'protector of the dharma.' To this day, the Reverend, members of the Sangha, and a handful of others linked to Willie during this time still call him Goho. The temple is affiliated with the Pure Land Buddhist community. Its world headquarters and original temple stand in the center of Old Kyoto, Japan. Both have stood in that spot for more than 850 years.

It was there, amidst the serene gardens and ancient halls, that Willie aspired to recenter himself, and to find solace and purpose. Remaining in his current situation felt perilous, a choice that threatened his very survival. Yes. For Willie, there was only one way to shed the burdens of the past five years: return to what he viewed as his source.

Kyoto beckoned with its ancient allure. The promise of deep meditation and profound quietude drew him in, offering a sanctuary where he could be truly alone. The mother temple, a place steeped in history and tranquility, called to him.

He would spend the next year meticulously planning his pilgrimage, crafting an itinerary that would take him far from the chaos of his current existence. He sought solitude, a reprieve from the cacophony that clanged in his spirit, and most importantly, a retreat from the distractions of grief, and of relationships...

Scene 6

An Ancient Memory

It was sometime in the long, slow year Willie spent preparing for his pilgrimage to Japan—somewhere between his daily meditation and his nightly unravellings—when Wasum, his young Thai neighbor, made an offhand observation that stuck with him longer than he'd admit.

"You and my aunt... you have the same spirit," she said one evening over beers and late conversation. "Same quiet, same vibe. Same knowing smile." Her aunt lived in Thailand, in a village so far-flung it barely cast a shadow. Wasum thought they might benefit from talking with each other—just simple chatter, she said, to see if anything clicked. Willie, still shell-shocked from the wreckage of Maria and clinging to his solitude like a life vest, shut the idea down cold. "No more women," he muttered, "Not even hypothetical ones." That was about eight, maybe nine months before he left on his trip. Long enough for the universe to get clever.

Willie and Wasum had one of those rare, peculiar connections that didn't lend itself to easy labels. It wasn't romance—not quite—but it wasn't platonic in the usual sense either. There was a kind of sophistication to it. Progressive, maybe. Quietly profound. Despite the twenty-year age gap and their stark contrast in style—Wasum with her polished, urban edge and Willie with his sun-worn denim and analog sensibilities—they met somewhere in the middle, on a wavelength few others could access.

She'd moved into the house next to Willie's RV some 18-months prior—the very same property he had rented years earlier from Tom, back when he needed four walls and a little distance from himself. Now, separated only by a hedge row and a sagging chain-link gate, Wasum arrived like some cosmic callback. She was vibrant, magnetic in that way some people just are—sharp-witted, sultry, and seemingly immune to the self-consciousness of youth. There was wisdom in her. The kind you earn early if you've seen enough of the world twist sideways. Willie took to her instantly, though he wouldn't have said so. And she, for reasons maybe only she fully understood, took to him.

She was fascinated by his dusty world—by his rituals, his dog-eared notebooks, his obsession with expired rolls of Kodak and shuttered light. She became his muse almost by accident, appearing again and again in his viewfinder: in the desert at golden hour, wandering old motels, draped in gauze by a bedroom window. Boudoir, desert noir, cigarette smoke curling through a shaft of sun. Art for the sake of it. Nothing more.

There was no infatuation, no crossed lines. Just something symbiotic. They'd finish each other's sentences and share a glance that said everything. It was the kind of bond that made traditional couples look clumsy by comparison.

Wasum had come to Cave Creek to escape a bad scene in the city—an ex who wouldn't stay gone. And Willie, in his way, was still nursing wounds that hadn't quite scabbed over. So they ran defense for each other. Looked out. Spent evenings on the porch sipping whiskey, swapping stories, dreaming out loud. They took road trips with no destination. Explored the dusty arteries of Arizona like outlaws on sabbatical.

Whatever they were, it worked. It held space for both of them. And maybe, in a quiet way, it made what happened next inevitable.

Now, unbeknownst to Willie—and this should surprise no one who knows him—Wasum had pulled a fast one on him during one of their nights out. Somewhere between a bourbon and the jukebox flickering out old Merle Haggard tunes, she'd taken his phone, installed WhatsApp, and quietly added her aunt's number to his contacts. Chitra. Then, with a twinkle in her eye and the mischief of a matchmaker, she passed Willie's number along to her aunt as well, encouraging her to reach out. A soft nudge from the universe, she called it.

What Wasum knew—and Willie didn't—is that Chitra never would. That's not how traditional Thai women operate, especially those of a certain age and bearing. The idea of initiating contact with a strange man was unthinkable, even if he came pre-approved by her distant niece.

So the whole thing should've just settled there—an idle app, a couple of unread numbers buried in a contact list. But fate, it seems, has fingers of its own.

A few mornings later, Willie found himself on his usual walk. Always the same trails, the same meandering loops he and Louie used to follow back when silence didn't feel so loud. On this particular day, something nudged him toward the Vortex—a winding path through a shallow desert valley, where the air felt charged with something older than language. Mesquite and palo verde trees gave way to monolithic boulders stacked in patterns that didn't make much geological sense, but somehow felt intentional. Like the gods had been building chess pieces and forgot to clean up.

He wandered through, alone but not lonely, inhaling that mineral-rich air and letting the stillness do its work. He made his way up and over a boulder and squeezed through into a little pocket where he always liked to sit. As he was about to sit on his favorite rock, cradled as if in the lap of Black Mountain, he heard it—a sound. Faint. Muffled. A voice?

He looked around. Again. This pocket of desert is usually empty, save for the lizards and ghosts. He instinctively glanced down and, out of habit more than logic, muttered, "Lou... where the hell's that voice coming from?"

Louie wasn't there, of course. But Willie still asked him things sometimes.

That's when he reached for his back pocket and pulled out his phone. The screen was glowing. He'd somehow, miraculously—or absurdly—pocket-dialed the very woman he was never supposed to call.

Chitra.

He stared at it for a second, unsure if he should hang up or apologize or just throw the damn thing into the desert and walk home. But before he could decide, a soft voice came through the speaker.

"Hello?" she said.

He froze. "Oh, wow—I... I'm so sorry. I didn't mean to call you!"

He paused. "Wasum," he muttered, like a man cursing a rain cloud that had just drenched his last dry cigarette.

She laughed—graceful, a little bashful. "Hello, Win", she said. *Win?* he thought to himself, *who the hell is Win... maybe she can't say Willie.*

They fumbled their way through introductions and soon unraveled the thread that connected them. Willie could tell instantly that Chitra was genuine, warm, even through the fractured bridge of their language. Her voice was gentle, but carried something...familiar, ancient. Not old—*timeless.*

Despite the hiccups of communication—half-sentences, guesses, laughter—they spoke. And then kept speaking. She told him a little about her family, her village, her ancestors—old landholders, medicine women, keepers of rice fields and stories. Her people were spread across Thailand like constellations: distant, proud, enduring.

Willie was still walking when the call started, but by the time he reached his RV, an hour had passed. And still they talked. Another hour, in fact. It was the kind of conversation that doesn't demand direction—it simply *is*.

When they finally hung up, he sat still for a moment, thumb hovering over the screen like it might disappear. Then he called Wasum. Told her what happened. Gave her hell. Then thanked her, too.

"It really was a great conversation," he said.

And knowing Willie, he meant it in that quiet, soul-level way of his—like a door cracked open just enough to let the light in.

It had been well over a year since Willie had seen Maria in person. They still spoke on the phone from time to time—Maria clinging to the frayed thread of something that once was, and Willie, ever the empath, unable—or unwilling —to sever it completely. I don't think he had the heart. Or maybe it was the spine he lacked. In truth, I think he was still trying to salvage some fragment of dignity between them, to figure out how to remain friends without crumbling under the weight of all that had passed. But he had made a pact with himself—three or four months prior, maybe more. No women. No distractions. Not until after Japan. Maybe. It was his clean break from the chaos, a vow carved in quiet desperation. And for once, he was sticking to it.

But the conversation with Chitra lingered.

Wasum, naturally, relayed her aunt's reflections after the call. She told Willie that Chitra had mentioned—more than once—the uncanny ease of the exchange, how they laughed easily, how the conversation felt... remembered, somehow. Not new. Familiar. As if it had been going on for centuries and they'd only just picked up the latest chapter. Chitra said—and this stuck with Willie, gnawed at him—that she felt their connection stretched back a thousand years, that she knew him already by the name *Win*. That kind of language wasn't metaphor for her. It was marrow. Cultural. Spiritual. Inborn. Willie tried to laugh it off, but the echo of it stayed with him.

Wasum had a photo on her phone. A few years old. Grainy. But even in low resolution, Chitra's beauty was undeniable—striking Thai features, high cheekbones, graceful posture, long raven hair cascading like a silk banner down her back. She was petite, elegant. The kind of woman who seemed carved by wind and time. Exactly the type Willie had always found himself undone by. And yet—he held fast. He'd only just begun piecing himself back together after the collapse of the Maria years, after losing Louie, after years of slow self-erasure. He wasn't about to derail that hard-earned progress for the ghost of a maybe.

And still... she stayed in his thoughts. Not loudly, but persistently. Like a whisper that refused to fade.

A few more days passed, and that same unnameable pull gnawed at him. A hum just beneath the skin. Willie couldn't shake it. He kept telling himself: What's the harm in a little conversation? She's 9,000 miles away. It's not like we're grabbing coffee at Janey's tomorrow. What's wrong with a friend? So he called. Told himself he'd keep it light. Casual. Said he just wanted to be friends—though who was he trying to convince, really?

They talked for hours. Again. Regularly.

There was that ease again. That uncanny fluency between them that didn't make a lick of sense. With Willie, less was always more when it came to women. For all his long-winded barroom yarns and front-porch philosophy, when it came to matters of the heart, he listened. He didn't over-explain himself. Didn't feel the need to. If someone couldn't intuit what he was about from the silence between his words, he figured it probably wasn't worth spelling out.

With Chitra, there was no pressure to perform. He let the conversations drift where they wanted. No real personal details, no confessions. He liked the safety of that distance. She was beautiful, yes. Striking even. But she lived in another world entirely. He could feel for her, even deeply, without worrying about falling too far.

But Chitra... she wasn't looking at this like some late-night call across oceans. She was a different kind of woman, anchored in traditions older than America itself. And she didn't need to tell Willie what she felt. That wasn't the way of things where she came from. You don't spill your heart at the first stirrings. You consult the ancestors. You burn incense. You kneel and listen.

So she did. As a confirmation. She spoke with her village's medicine woman. Sat with her father, a local sage. Visited monks at the temple. Prayed at shrines older than memory. And when she felt the answer whisper back through all those channels, she took one final step—down to the tattooist. An elder Phram who, after deep prayer and chanting, would ink visions from the gods onto the skin, not for decoration but for destiny. This was a critical ceremony in her old Isaan culture. It could sometimes mean the difference between life and death if not performed, or performed in misaligned timing.

She emerged with a red boat etched at the small of her back. A sign, the Phram told her, of someone known coming across great waters. She believed it was Willie. Not metaphorically. Not romantically. Spiritually. Viscerally. As certain as the sunrise. But she didn't tell him. That wasn't her way. This was between her, Buddha, and the gods. Willie was simply drifting toward something he couldn't yet name. But it was already in motion.

For several months, Chitra and Willie kept up a quiet rhythm of communication. Not daily, not performative, but steady—like two tide-worn stones occasionally knocking together in a riverbed. In Willie's mind, they were friends. Close ones. In Chitra's, they were already wed. That disparity—odd as it sounds—gave their connection a kind of purity. No pretense. No demands. It allowed their bond to form on something deeper than romance. Something closer to soul recognition.

I'll give Willie credit. He was sticking to his guns. In his younger years, he'd have been on the next flight out, probably married by Tuesday, divorced by Labor Day. But this time? He held the line. And I don't think it was willpower. I think the gods stepped in. I think they whispered, Not yet, not like this.

Because he was about to torpedo the whole thing and force it right out of his mind.

It was early June—maybe three months after that cosmic misdial had sparked it all—when Chitra, in her calm and reverent way, began to share more of what she felt. Just small pieces. How her ancestors whispered to her. How the village's spirit guides affirmed her sense that she and Willie were bound by lifetimes, not months. How the red boat tattooed on her back was a symbol, given through prayer, of his arrival. She wasn't trying to scare him. She was telling the truth as she understood it—unembellished, unpressured, but profoundly sincere.

Willie, for all his deep empathy, didn't handle it well. He panicked. Told her his life was upside down. That he was trying to rebuild from rubble. That he would never drag someone so serene and whole into his fractured world. He cut her off mid-thought. Shut the door before her words could finish settling in the room.

But she didn't protest. Didn't cry. Didn't accuse. Not her style.

She simply said, with a kind of soft certainty that unnerved him, "I understand, Win. But it's not up to us. It's already been written."

That quiet confidence? It rattled him. After five years of hurricanes with Maria—where every conversation was a collision—this woman's calm felt almost supernatural. *Who is this,* he wondered. And that scared him more than anything else.

So he did what scared men do. He faded.

Stopped calling. Stopped picking up. Every so often he'd respond to a message with something terse and apologetic: *My life is a mess. I can't be with you. Please understand.*

And she always answered the same way. *"Ok, Win. I understand. Don't worry."*

No bargaining. No bitterness. Just... regal elegance.

Weeks passed, then months. Every so often, Willie would get a message from Chitra. Just a few words. *Everything will turn out okay. I'll always be here, waiting.* That kind of grace sticks to a man's ribs. But eventually, even those stopped coming. No hard goodbye, no flurry of emotions—just a quiet tapering off, like the last notes of a song that knew not to overstay its welcome.

By then, Willie was locked in. There was a clarity to him I hadn't seen in years. He wasn't chasing epiphanies or trying to outrun heartbreak. He was on a mission. A resurrection, really. He was pulling himself out of the ashes with both hands, and Japan—of all places—was the forge. I couldn't help but wonder what he'd find there. Couldn't help but wonder if he'd come back at all.

He'd booked the trip nearly a year in advance. One of our friends—an international pilot—who coincidentally lived in Japan for several years and had a fondness for sake and well-timed advice—told him to look into multi-city bundles, the kind airlines quietly offer if you know how to dig. Sure enough, Willie found one through a Japanese carrier that included a leg up to Sapporo for a three-day detour. Oddly enough, it was cheaper than a straight round-trip ticket.

And—because when Willie goes in, he goes all in—he booked it business class. Last of his money. No regrets. If this was going to be the trip that reset his soul, he figured he might as well sip good whiskey and stretch his legs on the way to the fire.

Interesting thing about Willie, for all his fire and bravado—for the daredevil stunts, for the bar fights he avoided with wit and the women he couldn't—Willie Lyonsan was deathly afraid of flying. Not turbulence or hijackers or crashing in the Andes—though I'm sure he'd have made friends with the rescue dogs if it came to that. No, it was the sheer helplessness of it all. The sealed doors, the stale air, the lack of an exit strategy. Being boxed in, strapped down, trapped at 35,000 feet with no wheel in his hands and no way out? That's what got him.

Now if you let him *fly* the damn thing, he'd probably be fine. Probably. But sitting shoulder to shoulder with 300 strangers, packed in like cordwood for twelve hours or more? That was a whole other thing.

He knew this about himself. Had known for years. Eighteen or so, to be specific, when he flew to Hawaii with a woman he'd proposed to—on the beach, no less. She'd said yes, because of course she did. The man could sell rain to a thunderstorm. They made it to the islands just fine. Had a picture-perfect wedding. Then came the return leg.

Just as the inter-island jet was being pushed back towards the taxi way to take them from Maui to Oahu—just a quick 20-minute hop to the international terminal—Willie unraveled. Spectacularly. Hit the help light above like it owed him money. "Get me off this fucking plane right now!" he said, loud enough to earn glances and probably a few prayers. The flight attendant leaned toward the cockpit and spoke in hushed tones, but they were close enough to hear the pilot respond flatly.

"Bring the stairs back. Get him off."

So they did. Bride and groom, still sun-kissed and lei-wrapped, walked back down the steps and into the terminal like two characters in a romantic comedy that had veered sharply into absurdist drama. Willie turned to her and said, with absolute sincerity, "We're gonna have to get jobs and move here. Because I'm never getting back on another goddamn plane."

Six hours later, after a Xanax and a few pep talks from deeply compassionate airport staff who had clearly seen it all, he was airborne again. No incident. No freak-out. Just Willie, silent as the clouds, gripping the armrests with white knuckles and a vow never to speak of it again.

Until now, of course.

Maria. Lou. The devastating losses. The fallout. The tumble that teetered too close to the abyss. It was all ever-present in his psyche like a spirit cloud, but he was in a much different head space. Focused. The pilgrimage, the reset, the promise of resurrection, it was all bigger than any flight. Because the truth is, even the biggest spirits get caged by something. And for Willie, that something came with a boarding pass.

Scene 7

It All Fell Away

What had once felt like a distant idea—almost a year out—soon became months, then weeks, and finally days away. Time didn't pass; it dissolved. From the moment Willie booked the trip, it was as if the universe had hit fast-forward. And true to form, he met the countdown with a kind of fervent precision that would make an accountant sob with gratitude. He mapped out his pilgrimage with a detail so exacting it could've earned him honorary mention in *Travel + Leisure*—or at the very least, a polite bow from Rick Steves.

Though Willie loathed structure in most areas of his life—schedules made his skin crawl—he approached the logistics of this journey with monastic devotion. Japan had become his second language, not in speech, but in movement. Over the past year, he'd memorized train maps and station layouts like a gambler memorizes tells. The Shinkansen lines, the MRT webbing—he'd cartographed them in his mind like a sacred text. He could tell you which platform in Shinagawa Station would get you to Gifu with a six-minute transfer in Nagoya, and where to stand to catch the car that opened closest to the station stairs. It was borderline obsessive. But he wasn't just prepared—he was tuned in, already halfway there in spirit. And while still a monumental leap, the state of Willie's spirit leading up to the jump off point, made the flights a mere formality. Though, he drilled those until they became part of his muscle memory too.

Two days before liftoff, Willie grabbed his backpack and slung another small fanny pack over his shoulder—the sum total of what he was taking to Japan—and drove to Old Town to stay with his old friend Suzi. She lived ten minutes from the airport and a thousand miles from the noise in his head. Suzi wasn't just a friend; they shared the same birthday, the same oddball timing, the same restless, generous spirit. Her home was like a temple wrapped in adobe and lavender. Quiet. Still. Sacred. The kind of place where even your thoughts speak softer. It was the right move

—his nerves were humming like power lines, and he needed a place to come down gently before the flight.

That night, a breeze from the past blew in wearing a velvet soul and a warm smile. One of their mutual friends, Roxy—deeply spiritual, unnervingly intuitive, a woman Willie had once briefly dated back when life was a little less bruised—showed up out of nowhere to stay the night. No agenda. Just beauty. The three of them walked into the heart of Old Town Scottsdale, shared a few drinks, traded old stories and new laughter, and slowly turned the volume of the world all the way down.

Back at Suzi's, they each found their corners of peace. No drama. No goodbyes. Just stillness. Willie's flight was set to leave at 7 a.m.—which meant a 4:30 a.m. wake-up and a quiet ride through the empty, dark desert to Sky Harbor. It was, in hindsight, the perfect sendoff. Not some grand fireworks farewell. Just a soft letting go. A gentle exhale before the plunge.

Willie's itinerary had him routing through San Francisco first—a short hop to the coast before the long haul across the Pacific.

Phoenix Sky Harbor – San Francisco International
Flight Number NH7307
Departure: 7:05 AM
Seat: 01A
Flight Time: 2 hours
Distance: 707 miles

Of course, Willie had everything mapped and measured down to the minute. That was his way now—ritual as survival. As Suzi's car wheeled up to the curb outside Terminal 3, they came to a slow, quiet stop. Hugs were exchanged, soft and unceremonious, the kind you give when there's too much left unsaid and no time left to say it. Then he was off—through the terminal, through security, through that in-between space where you float without tether until the gate agent calls your number.

And despite it all—the wreckage he was hauling around inside him like a duffel full of bricks—Willie was still. No nerves. No dread. No cold sweats. The man who once had to be peeled off a puddle jumper in Hawaii because his pulse outran his courage now sat at Gate B4 calm as lake water. Strangely, almost unnervingly, he couldn't wait to get on the plane.

He watched through the thick terminal glass as the sunrise flared against the tarmac, jet engines kicking up heat mirage. Something rose up in him—not hope exactly, but something akin to it. A quiet knowing. A foretelling. The moment those wheels left the ground, everything that had broken him over the last half-decade—Maria's unraveling, Louie's passing, the quiet war inside him—would stay earthbound. That was the bargain he'd struck with the universe. He'd leave his ghosts in the terminal and take only his bones with him. And somewhere, high over the Pacific, he'd begin stitching himself back together.

Not whole, maybe. But something close enough to begin again.

Boarding was quiet. Uneventful. No frantic gate changes or crying toddlers or men in flip-flops shouting into speakerphones. Just a kind of hush, like the hush that precedes something sacred. His seat mate—already tucked into her aisle seat—was mid-movie on her iPad, earbuds in, face softly lit by the flickering screen. Willie offered a courteous nod as he eased into the window seat, careful not to jostle her. She smiled, paused her movie, and within minutes they were chatting.

She was a bank executive. Recently back from a trip to Italy with her husband. They'd fallen in love with

Florence. Willie said something charming about Michelangelo's David and managed not to sound like a guy who'd Googled it in the boarding line. By the time they finished exchanging travel tales and middle names, they might as well have known each other ten years. Willie had that effect. He was never long without a friend.

With the last bags stowed and the safety demo dutifully ignored, the plane pushed off the gate and began to taxi. Still no anxiety. Willie was calm—eerily so, given his well-documented distaste for air travel. Willie glanced at his seat mate's leg now bouncing a subtle but steady rhythm as the nose turned to face the runway. The engines spooled up, and they were off like a promise chasing its own tail.

Out the window, the familiar landmarks of Phoenix peeled away beneath. The curved brown ridges of the Papagos, the maze of suburban rooftops, the tidy tyranny of HOA-approved neighborhoods. Then: sprawl gave way to dust, dust to desert, desert to sky as they punched through a gauzy veil of cloud and leveled out.

Willie settled back in his seat and searched the corners of his spirit for the feeling of release he'd prophesied on the ground...it wasn't there.

The flight attendant came by with a snack basket and a worn-out smile. A packet of peanuts was dropped on each of their trays, followed by drink orders.

"Coke," Willie said. He wasn't usually a soda guy—too sweet, too fizzy—but his throat had made the call for something with bubbles. As he sipped the half can of coke he was given in a plastic glass full of ice, he glanced at the peanuts, then at the small brass plaque above that read *First Class,* then at his seat mate.

"I know," she said.

"You're going to be floored by the difference once you're on the international leg," she added, with the certainty of someone who's seen things.

"Let's hope so," Willie said. They both chuckled.

The flight labored on. He found an opening between snack trays and other passengers to use the restroom, and settled back in his seat for the last 40 minutes of this leg.

Then, somewhere over the ragged peaks of the Sierra Nevada, it hit him.

Not like a thunderbolt. Not a panic. Not a vision. But something quieter. A shift in air pressure, like the cabin had filled with a different kind of oxygen—cleaner, lighter, almost holy. That feeling he'd hoped for on the ground, the one he tried to will into existence back at the gate? It arrived unannounced and filled him like a tide.

Relief. Real, bone-deep, soul-level relief.

It moved through him like music. The tension that had choked his spirit for the better part of the last decade— the ache of Maria, the ghost of Louie, the hollowing out of a man who once believed in everything—unspooled and fell away, like old armor slipping from his shoulders into the Sequoia's below.

He didn't cry. But if he had, no one would've blamed him.

As the plane gradually dipped into its final descent, almost silent over the Bay, the wheels touched down as soft as a whisper. And as they taxied toward the gate, a voice— clear and sure, not his own—rose up from somewhere inside and said:

Things are different now.

Willie blinked, swallowed, and realized his palms were soaked. So was the collar of his shirt. He looked like he'd just run a mile through monsoon season. But inside? He felt rinsed clean.

Three hours till the next flight. A business class ticket bought him full access to the Polaris Lounge. And after everything he'd just shed 30,000 feet above California, he figured he'd earned every amenity they had on offer.

Having never flown like this before, Willie approached one of the attendants in the lounge with that signature blend of earnestness and misplaced thrift that made him so damn endearing.

"Where do I pay for these?" he asked, eyeing the elegant buffet of juices, fresh coffee, ripe fruit, flaky pastries, and breakfast sandwiches laid out with all the quiet confidence of a five-star brunch spread.

The attendant smiled kindly. "They're complimentary, sir."

Willie blinked, nodded like he didn't want to seem too surprised, and grabbed a coffee and a Danish—just one, though he stared at a second long enough to make it blush. He settled into a wide, overstuffed chair beside a window overlooking the tarmac. The sunrise played tricks on the planes outside, and for a rare moment, he let himself sink into the feeling—new, clean, unrushed. If purgatory had a lobby like this, he thought, nobody'd be in a hurry to reach heaven.

That's when he noticed it: a tall pair of glass doors off to one side, with a silver plaque that read simply *Showers*. He instinctively inhaled the collar of his shirt—standard

Willie protocol—and winced. "Well, hell," he muttered. "Why not."

Still riding high on the strange gravity of this new version of himself, he wandered over and approached the front desk like a man checking into a weekend spa retreat.

"I'd like a shower, please, ma'am," he said in a tone that split the difference between Thurston Howell III and a rodeo drifter trying to impress the concierge.

"Yes, sir," she said with practiced elegance, leading him down a polished hallway lined with soft lighting and too-expensive wood paneling. She opened a door to a private suite that looked more like a high-end hotel room than anything he'd seen inside an airport.

"Here you are. Take your time. Help yourself to any of the toiletries—right over there." She gestured to a silver tray, where soaps, shampoos, lotions, and tiny bottles of something called "facial elixir" were arranged like relics from a future Willie hadn't planned on entering.

Inside, he stared at the gleaming fixtures and rain-style shower head like he'd stumbled into Narnia. He peeled off the travel grime and five years of heartache, letting the hot water work on him like a second baptism. By the time he emerged, steam trailing behind him, his dome freshly shaved and glowing like a jazz musician after last call, he looked more like a man on the first day of his new life than someone halfway to Tokyo.

He walked back through the lounge, grabbed an orange juice this time—something about Vitamin C felt appropriate—and made his way to the gate. His next ride? A 787-9 Dreamliner. The name alone sounded like a prophecy. His seat, dubbed *The Room*, and it was exactly that: a pod with a lay-flat bed, a privacy door, a 24-inch screen, and a meal service that would put some white-linen restaurants to shame.

They handed him a leather amenities kit with slippers, an eye mask, noise-canceling headphones, a travel toothbrush, and an array of elegant potions he'd never heard of but now, apparently, owned. He held the bag like it might grant him three wishes.

This was not the beginning of a trip. This was a threshold. A departure not just from Phoenix, or San Francisco, or even the ghosts that had trailed him all these years.

This was the opening act of something holy.

San Francisco International - Tokyo Narita
Flight Number NH7
Departure: 12:00 PM

Seat: 07A
Flight Time: 11 hours, 20 minutes
Distance: 5,599 miles

Willie settled into his "room"—there's no other word for it—
and let out a long breath, the kind that leaks from your soul
when something inside you finally unclenches. If the Polaris
Lounge was the velvet handshake, this Dreamliner was the
cathedral.

The moment he sank into that seat—lie-flat buttons,
private, appointed with all the fixings of a man who'd made
better life choices—he felt that peculiar stillness deepen.
Like something had opened inside him just wide enough to
let in a bit of grace.

His previous seat mate had promised this would be a
different experience entirely, and she wasn't wrong. The
flight attendants—resplendent in their crisp, orchid-
trimmed uniforms—moved with a balletic precision that
defied gravity and jet lag alike. Willie told me they glided
around the cabin like they were born of silk and intention,
communicating in graceful nods and hands placed just so,
one appearing the moment before the other disappeared.
Like some kind of airborne tea ceremony designed to lower
your blood pressure.

And then—*wait, this is a rear-facing seat*, he mused.

He hadn't noticed at first. Too caught up in the miniature universe around him—the menus, the slippers, the way the light hit the polished accents of his little flying apartment. But once he did, he grinned. *I'll be damned,* he thought. Facing backward. It fit. After the last few years, what better way to barrel into the future than looking at where you'd just been?

He wasn't facing anyone directly. In fact, it was just his row up against a bulkhead to the rear of the galley that was aft facing. His seat had a window, two in fact, and an aisle—a thin slice of quiet between him and the rest of the world. The solitude suited him. He told me later it felt like riding in reverse through everything he'd carried up to this point. As if the flight itself was a symbolic extraction: pulling him out of a life that had done its best to swallow him whole and sending him into one where maybe—just maybe—he could breathe again.

The plane was a monster, that much he knew from the window in San Francisco. A flying city. Willie said he couldn't wrap his head around how something so massive could lift into the sky, but lift it did. When the engines opened up on the runway and the Dreamliner launched forward like a slingshot, he felt it in his bones. The strange pull of physics pressed him gently forward in that rear-facing seat, and for a split second he thought: *This is what starting over feels like.*

Then the nose tilted, the ground slipped away, and the ocean opened its wide blue throat. Through the thick pane of reinforced glass, he watched the coast peel away below him, the California shoreline vanishing into haze and memory. Cities receded like regrets. Roads turned to veins. The past, it seemed, was shrinking behind him, mile by mile.

And with every thousand feet of altitude, something more fell away. Another part of the ache. Another shard of Louie's loss. Another remnant of the Maria storm that had torn up his life like a twister through the prairie.

He told me it was like watching all the broken pieces of himself dislodge, tumble off the plane, and plummet into the Pacific below—softly, like ash. He imagined them scattering across the water, swallowed up by the tide. Nothing left but salt and sky.

Sublime, he called it.

And with a stark realization he was a giant leap closer to the soul reset he set out on. This leg would actually take him *to Japan.* During that flight he said he felt his soul resetting its compass midair.

Save for a few polite shivers of turbulence spaced out like commas, the flight was exactly what Willie needed it to be—a reprieve from the world, wrapped in altitude and silence. The food was unlike anything he'd ever had, at 35,000 feet or elsewhere. Artfully plated, absurdly flavorful. Three full meals, plus an open invitation to indulge in snacks or spirits whenever the mood struck. Willie, never one to abuse hospitality but also never one to ignore it, opted for a few extra-dry Asahi's—crisp, cold, and served with the kind of reverence you'd expect in a proper izakaya tucked down an alley in Osaka.

He watched a few movies. Napped. Opened his MacBook and pecked out fragments of prose—half-thoughts, haiku-stained journal entries, little meditations on motion and memory. He didn't push it. Didn't try to wring brilliance from the altitude. He just wrote what came.

Somewhere around the midpoint of the flight, the cabin softened. The lights dimmed. Curtains were drawn. Flight attendants floated through the aisles, helping passengers convert their pods into beds—tight corners transformed into cocoons. A ballet of bedding and whispered instructions. Willie followed suit, folding himself into his private space with the slow, practiced movements of someone unwrapping something precious.

One pillow tucked beneath his head. Another pulled close to his chest like an old lover he never got to say goodbye to. And there he lay, long and low, wrapped in warmth and altitude and silence.

He slept.

Not the light doze of travel-weary tourists or the neck-cricked desperation of coach sleepers, but a true sleep. A deep, cleansing kind. Willie said later it felt like hibernation, like his soul had slipped beneath the ice for a few quiet hours to heal in the dark. He dreamed of Japan— not the Google version with beaches and lanterns, but something ancient. Monks in saffron robes. Temple bells echoing through cedar forests. Peace. Not as a concept, but as a presence.

When he woke, the lights were still low, the hush still intact. He reoriented his little room—seat upright, tray stowed—and stared quietly out the window at a sea of clouds drifting slow beneath them like ghost ships. He asked for another Asahi. The attendant bowed and returned a moment later with an open can, condensation just beginning to bead.

Turning back towards the window, he saw it.

Not dramatically, not with any cinematic swell of music—but simply, like it had always been there, waiting for him. The coastline of Japan. Soft. Dreamlike. An ink-brushed landscape unfurling beneath the wing.

He didn't gasp. Didn't weep. Just sat there, watching, feeling something in his chest unfurl too. It was beautiful—yes—but it was more than that. It felt like a painting, sure. But more like a memory he hadn't made yet. Something sacred that had been tucked away for him.

And the voice—that same voice he heard whisper through his bones when he landed in San Francisco—came again. This time deeper, clearer. *Things are different now.*

As the Dreamliner glided across the coastline, on a slow, gradual descent into Japan's open palm, Willie watched the countryside come to life. Villages like specks of calligraphy. Roadways threading through green. It was like watching a story take shape—one he hadn't written yet, but one he knew was his.

And in that moment, he didn't feel the absence of pain, or the simple relief of escape.

He felt beginnings.

That rare, holy feeling that your life isn't ending—it's just turning the page.

The giant plane eased onto the runway and made a dramatic brake to a slow roll to the gate. He arrived.

For the next 30 days, Willie explored Japan like a man trying to memorize a symphony—note by note, movement by movement, letting it seep into him. He didn't approach the country like a tourist ticking boxes. He moved like a pilgrim. Or maybe a ghost, retracing a life he might have lived in another time.

He knelt on tatami mats in temples older than the idea of America. Sat beneath paper lanterns that cast soft halos over steaming bowls of ramen so complex they could've been classified as poetry. He wandered Kyoto like a man under a spell, walking its narrow alleyways and cobblestone backstreets with reverence—eyes up, heart open. He bowed to monks, to shopkeepers, to the rising sun itself.

In Nara, he fed crackers to the sacred deer who bowed in return, their soft, unblinking eyes holding something ancient. In Inari, he climbed the endless tunnel of crimson toriis, each gate like a beat in a meditative drumline, rising through the trees and winding up the mountain until the city fell away and all that remained was breath, and wood, and wind. He stood still in Nagano as the snow monkeys soaked in hot springs and gave him a side-eye that suggested they'd seen men like him come and go for centuries.

In Hiroshima, he walked with his head low, heart heavy. He said the silence there was louder than any city he'd ever known. And in Osaka, he drank highballs and neat pours of Yamazaki, letting the caramel heat burn away things he didn't have names for. Somewhere along the way he tasted grilled eel so tender it made him swear under his breath, and sipped a yuzu cocktail that caught him off guard with its grace. Japan didn't just feed you. It seduced you. Slowly. Thoroughly.

There were moments of flirtation, too. Subtle. Gentle. A barista in a Kyoto café who complimented his film camera and lingered a little longer than necessary. A waitress in Osaka who laughed at his attempt to order in Japanese and then brought him a drink he didn't ask for but loved. Willie never pursued any of them. He was still keeping his vow. But it was nice to feel seen again, even fleetingly. To feel like a man and not a husk.

He rode the Shinkansen like it was a chariot—silent, smooth, faster than thought—staring out at rice paddies and mist-covered mountains like they were postcards from a calmer universe. He took photos constantly. Not to post. Not to prove. But to try and pin down the pulse of the country before it slipped through his fingers. He said it felt like

Japan had cracked him open and was gently putting the pieces back, rearranged, maybe even upgraded.

By the end of the month, his gait had changed. Slower, more deliberate. He spoke less. Smiled more. He'd learned a few dozen words in Japanese and used them with sincerity.

The man who boarded the plane in Phoenix with a fractured soul was still fractured—but now the pieces were starting to hum in harmony.

And then... Tokyo.

He would spend his last three days and two nights there—catch an event, explore the gardens, maybe wander a back alley bar or two, before heading back home. There was a rhythm to Tokyo that was different—edgier, faster. Willie could feel it in the sidewalk under his boots. It buzzed through neon signs and echoed in the way strangers moved past each other without touching. It was electric. And maybe just a little dangerous.

He messaged me that morning: *Tokyo's different. Feels like the volume's been turned up.*

That was the last normal message I got.

The rest of the story?

Well, you've already seen the start of it. A man stumbling down a dark alley, his memory swallowed whole, gravity failing, phone gone, shirt damp with sweat. A fall that looked like the end—but was really just the door swinging open on the next chapter.

Because Tokyo didn't break Willie. Not exactly.

It just... rerouted him.

Right into the heart of madness, mystery, and something else entirely.

Thailand.

But let's not jump too far ahead. Not just yet.

Let's pick up, now, where we left him—blinking under fluorescent lights, reaching for a bottle of water he'd never drink, just before the world spun completely off its axis. There are a few questions here begging for answers.

Scene 8

The Tokyo Incident

Willie spent his final two nights in Tokyo with a serene sort of punctuation mark—like the whole trip had ended on a soft exhale. His flight wasn't scheduled to depart until 9:05 p.m., which gave him an additional full day to wander the city that had, strangely, started to feel like a second skin.

He woke early, refreshed. Showered. Hauled his backpack to the curb and flagged down a cab in front of the hotel. The driver, polite and quiet, whisked him away through the winding arteries of the city while Willie sipped a perfectly aromatic hotel coffee and let the morning glide past the window. He had a plan for the day, casual but complete —exactly the kind of intentional loafing he'd perfected by now. Check in, get his boarding pass, walk to Haneda Shrine, soak up the ocean air at Jonanjima Seaside Park, grab a late lunch, head back and browse the airport's legendary shops before drifting toward his gate.

The cab let him off at Terminal 3. The place was practically empty. Serene. In a strange way, it felt like the universe was still cradling him—like it wanted this journey to end on a whisper, not a bang.

The All Nippon Airways counter stood almost directly ahead. No line. A beautiful young attendant greeted him with a bright smile. Willie handed over his passport with the air of a man who was already imagining himself in seat 01A —Asahi in hand, slippers on, stretched out in "The Room" and watching the moonlight paint the sky over the Pacific.

Tokyo Haneda to Los Angeles LAX
Flight NH126
Departure: 9:05 p.m.
Arrival: 2:05 p.m. (same day)
Seat: 01A
Flight Time: 11 hr

As she typed away, Willie's mind wandered forward—to Cave Creek. He imagined pulling up to his place, dust in the air, later maybe catching the last strains of a band playing down at Harold's. He felt good. He felt ready. In that moment, he told himself, he was going home whole.

But then came the hiccup.

The smile on the attendant's face faltered, just slightly. "I'm sorry, sir," she said, "it appears your ticket has been canceled."

Willie blinked. "I'm sorry... what?"

She pointed gently to her screen. "You were scheduled to board a flight to Sapporo on the ninth. You didn't check in. Under our policy, that's considered a no-show. When that happens, the rest of the itinerary is automatically voided."

Willie's mouth moved before his brain caught up. "I had no idea. I thought I could just skip that leg. I didn't realize it would cancel the rest." He tried to steady his voice. "Is there any way to fix it? I paid a lot for that seat."

"I'm very sorry, sir. There's nothing I can do here."

She bowed, soft and final.

And just like that, the end of the journey turned into a fork in the road.

Willie stepped away from the counter slowly, like a man waking up from a beautiful dream only to find the alarm clock blinking 12:00. He took a breath, counted to three, and let the inner monologue roll:

Alright, keep it together. This is just another turn in the story. You're not on a schedule. You're not in crisis. Not anymore. You're okay. You're strong. You're good. So... what now?

He checked his account on his phone—over budget by a heap the yen was perilously close to bare. No return flight. No backup plan. But standing in that polished terminal, beneath signs in kanji and the scent of warm dorayaki from a nearby stall, Willie didn't feel panic. He felt... curious.

This wasn't a setback. It was a plot twist.

And for a man like Willie Lyonsan, plot twists were just invitations to lean in a little more.

He called his mom back in Michigan to let her know the latest installment of the Willie Lyonsan Odyssey: stuck in Tokyo, ticketless, but strangely serene about it. No panic in his voice, no shame in the predicament—just a kind of amused curiosity, like the universe had paused the film and handed him the script with a wink.

"Don't worry," he told her, "I've been in tighter spots with less." And he meant it. He had a little money left—not enough for a flight, but enough for a bed, a few bowls of noodles, and a few more stories to tuck away.

He wasn't about to ask his parents for a bailout. They were on fixed incomes and he'd rather sleep in the airport than put that kind of pressure on them. Instead, he phoned his buddy in Cave Creek—the pilot, the one who helped book the multi-city ticket in the first place. He might have some ideas.

"Jesus, Willie," the guy said, "Say the word and I'll wire you what you need."

It was a kind offer. A good offer. But Willie waved it off—for now. Mixing money and friendship was like mixing whiskey and milk: fine in theory, tragic in practice. It was enough to know the option existed. That alone gave him room to breathe, to lean into the moment like maybe—just maybe—this was supposed to happen.

The universe doesn't always send angels. Sometimes it sends delays and cancellations and busted itineraries.

And so, he pivoted.

He cracked open his laptop, scanned for last-minute lodging, and landed on a capsule hotel just across the street from the Oriental Express, where he'd stayed the two nights prior. He liked that stretch of town—knew the streets, the rhythm, the way the vending machines hummed at night like distant cicadas. For thirty U.S. bucks, it was a no-brainer. He booked two nights, just in case.

He skipped the shrine, bypassed the seaside park, and made his way back toward familiar ground.

The capsule hotel was exactly what it claimed to be: a pod. A tiny horizontal coffin of serenity, lined with pressed board and possibility. Willie climbed up, stretched out, and stared at the ceiling for a while before cracking his knuckles and getting back to work. There was always a way forward. He just had to find it.

With late afternoon approaching his stomach piped up. Time for dinner. *This puzzle will live to see another day.* He put it out of his mind, stowed his things, dropped to the floor like a paratrooper, headed out the door and rounded the corner toward the Oriental Express. The city was already beginning to take on its early evening tone—neon signs flickering awake, salarymen loosening ties, the smell of grilled yakitori seeping from tiny alley kitchens. He turned and walked into the lobby.

The clerk he'd befriended—a soft-spoken woman with an easy smile and a no-nonsense bun—was behind the desk.

"Back so soon?" she asked, raising an eyebrow.

"Turns out," Willie said, "I'm not quite finished with Japan."

She laughed. He gave her the thumbnail version of the airline mishap, shrugged it off with the charm of a man who's either lost his mind or found his peace.

Then he slipped back into the Tokyo dusk to hunt down something familiar, something cheap, and something distinctly Japanese—because if the universe was insisting he stay, the least he could do was order seconds.

A short walk from the Oriental Express—quicker still if you cut through the alley—was a little tavern Willie had taken a real shine to. One of those blink-and-you-miss-it joints, local to the marrow. Inside, a slim bar hugged the left wall with maybe eight stools, worn smooth by regulars. Opposite that, four small tables stood in a soldierly line, two chairs apiece, their wood lacquered with decades of soy sauce, laughter, and spilled secrets. On the far end—where you had to tilt your whole spine to see it—hung a single, flickering TV. Baseball. Always baseball. The bartender, a rather tall Tokyo lifer with a penchant for conversation and a deep love for the Yomiuri Giants, had owned the place for twenty years. His English wasn't perfect, but it was better than Willie's Japanese, and the man poured whiskey like it was church communion. If there wasn't a live game on, he was playing an old one—old baseball footage looping like a memory. The kind of place you don't find so much as get found by.

Right next door was a little restaurant. The waitress in there looked like she'd retired her smile sometime around the late 80s. Ornery as a cactus. Willie had eaten there twice before, both times trying to tease out even the smallest grin. No dice. But this time, as he stepped through the door— having said a soft, unanswered farewell the night before— something in her posture shifted. Maybe it was the way the afternoon light hit his face. Maybe it was the way he bowed. Whatever it was, he caught it: the hint of a smirk that wasn't entirely hostile. "Konichiwa," Willie said, smiling like a man with nowhere better to be. She pointed at an empty table without a word.

And I'll be damned—when he sat down and glanced toward the window, he caught her reflection in the glass. She was smiling.

"Yakiniku Donburi?" she asked without looking up.

"Hai," Willie nodded, his grin softening into something real.

Just then, the bell above the door jingled, and in walked two familiar faces. They slid into a booth like regulars. Willie recognized them instantly from the night before at the baseball tavern—two guys who'd stood out not just for their friendliness, but for that unspoken quality that says, we're good people, trust us. A nod. A smile. That effortless rapport.

"Thought you were flying out," said the taller one— the pharmacist, if Willie remembered right.

"Little delay," Willie said, patting his chest. "Long story."

They shared a knowing chuckle, that quick bond of strangers who had, for a few hours at least, not been strangers at all. Turns out they'd hit it off harder than Willie realized. Both men were in their thirties, sharp but unpretentious. The pharmacist was thoughtful and precise, the kind of man who measured words before using them. The other, hat backwards and velvet grin, was a semi-famous pop star in Japan—not household, but enough that heads turned when he walked into a place. Willie had no clue, of course, until they'd parted ways the first time and the bartender filled him in.

As Willie worked through the last few bites of his meal, the pop star leaned over the table with a casual proposition. "We wanted to take you around last night," he said, "give you a proper send-off. A real Japanese yokocho experience. Still got time?"

"Yokocho?" Willie asked.

"It means alleyway," the pharmacist explained. "Where the real izakayas live. The good stuff. Not the tourist joints."

Willie raised an eyebrow. He didn't need convincing. Experience was the one thing he never turned down.

"Sounds fun," he said with a grin. "Lead the way."

They hit the alleys like old friends with a shared past instead of three men whose stories had only barely overlapped. The yokocho was everything they promised— tight backstreets lit by paper lanterns and the low hum of a thousand conversations, punctuated by the hiss of yakitori on open coals and the occasional drunken laugh skipping across puddles of spilled sake. These weren't the polished restaurants from the guidebooks. These were tucked away living rooms with a liquor license, where you had to know someone to stay, the table legs wobbled and the stories were older than the barstools themselves.

The pop star—RYO Tanaka from the group Ketsumeishi—was greeted like a long-lost brother everywhere they went. Heads turned, jaws dropped, and at more than one stop, girls squealed like the Beatles had just materialized out of a puff of shochu vapor. But the man never soaked in the adoration. Instead, he pulled Willie tighter into the spotlight, introducing him like some

mysterious American auteur who'd shown up to shoot a
documentary on the soul of Tokyo nightlife. "He's a
photographer," he'd say, "but really, he's a poet." Willie,
modest as ever, would just nod and lift his glass.

And not once—not once—did they let him pay. Not for
a drink, not for a skewer of grilled mackerel, not even for the
hot towel they handed him between bars. At each stop,
drinks materialized in front of him like conjuring tricks. If
his glass dipped below half, someone refilled it. If he reached
for the bottle, a hand gently stopped him. "You are our
honored guest," the pharmacist said at one point. "And our
elder." That last word made Willie laugh. The kid was maybe
thirty-one.

They spoke in a blend of English, Japanese, and what
Willie later called "drunk dialect"—that slurred, universal
shorthand where gestures did most of the talking. They
laughed without a care, toasted to music, to brotherhood, to
America, to late trains and missed planes and second
chances.

Eventually, after four or five bars and countless
toasts, they wound back toward the neighborhood near
Willie's capsule hotel. The pop star's fans were still
whispering behind their phones when he gave Willie a hug
and said, "You changed my view of Americans." The

pharmacist bowed deeply, then reached out and squeezed Willie's shoulder like they'd known each other since the sandbox. With a final wave, they turned and disappeared into the electric haze of Tokyo's midnight.

Willie, buzzed but lucid, wandered back toward the baseball tavern. The neon flickered like it was trying to wink him inside. He stepped in, nodded at the bartender, and settled onto a stool for one more like a man slipping into his element. Then he saw her—Famica.

She was perched at the end of the bar, drink in hand, smile already forming before he even looked her way. She'd been there the night before, small talk and glances, nothing much. But now she looked up at him like he was the encore she hadn't expected. "You came back," she said.

Willie smiled. "I guess I wasn't finished."

She slid over a few inches, just enough to close the distance but leave a whisper of mystery between them. The bartender placed another whiskey in front of him without asking.

And here, dear reader, is where the shadows began to lean in.

Willie still had his wits. He knew his limits. But Famica had other plans. She didn't come just to drink. She came with a different kind of thirst. The kind that curls into your ear and makes you forget what time it is. The kind that lets you think you're steering, while she's already chosen the destination. A couple more drinks. A closer lean. Her hand briefly on his thigh. Just enough contact to make him feel welcome, just enough mystery to keep him guessing.

To be sure, the night began to slide right here—slowly at first, like a glass too close to the table's edge.

And Willie, bless him, didn't see it coming. Not yet.

He was just far enough removed from his wits—and the promise he'd made to himself—tilted just enough off the rhythm he'd built to the point of the cosmic reroute of the cancelled flight, that he started looking at her differently. Noticing, nay, studying the sweep of hair that draped over one eye and across her cheek like a sigh of vulnerability. Taking in, perhaps too late, the low line of her blouse and the single pearl resting just beneath it, catching light like a secret. Famica was the picture of Japanese elegance—poised, enigmatic, a little too perfect. And Willie? Willie was neck-deep now, floating in a moment that felt warm and ageless. The clarity he'd carried 24 hours earlier had dissolved like sugar in hot tea. He wasn't thinking of promises or plans. He was untethered. No watch. No compass. Just a man adrift, and damn the consequences.

What he didn't see—or couldn't through the haze of the celestial moment he was in—was the mirage forming just outside his line of sight. Famica wasn't alone in this little theatre of misdirection. There was a quiet choreography at play. The bartender knew her, that much was clear. And just beyond the reach of the bar light, a third player sat against the far wall—half-shadowed, unreadable. Willie had clocked him moments before, in passing, on the way to the bathroom. He'd been there the night before too. But tonight, Willie wasn't quite himself. His radar was dim.

When he returned back at the bar, Famica resumed her gentle pull. That subtle gravity of proximity. Willie, to his credit, had already decided he was done drinking. Nearly 50 years I'd known the man—never once had he crossed the line between controlled looseness and genuine intoxication. But something was off. Way off.

He planned to finish his drink, say something slick and maybe follow her lead—see where the night wanted to end. But just as he turned to speak, the ground shifted beneath him. Not metaphorically—literally. The bar pitched sideways like the whole world had slipped its axis. The floor moved in fragments, the lights smeared across his vision like oil on water. He blinked hard, forced a smile like nothing was wrong, and fixed his eyes on the door, trying to find something—anything—to hold his balance.

What the hell is happening? he thought. This isn't booze. I know what a buzz feels like. This is something else.

He bolted. No goodbye. No explanation. Just muscle memory and survival instinct. Like a thoroughbred at The Preakness loosed from the gates, he lunged for the door.

And then—Darkness.

It's hard to piece the timeline together exactly—too many missing frames, too much static on the reel. But from what Willie later managed to reconstruct, somewhere between the moment his mind slipped into the dark and the faint, dreamlike glimpse of the Oriental Express sign flickering like a candle in a fishbowl, he somehow, by divine muscle memory or cosmic grace, managed to call Wasum.

What he said, if anything, was unintelligible. Just the sound of him, warped and distant, like a voice pulled through three dimensions—like he was phoning from underwater in a different timeline. That's how she described it. His words were not words, but feeling. Instinct. A distress flare launched into the unknown.

And from there—well, we know now what he didn't know then: that invisible strings tied to something far more divine than logic intervened. That fate, God, karma, ancestors, ghosts, or whatever name you want to give the hands behind the curtain pulled him from the ledge of certain doom and smuggled his spirit out of Japan. Had they not? Best case, he'd be nursing a weeklong hospital stay. Worst case? Front-page headline. A confused, foreign man in custody. A face on the evening news. A footnote in someone else's cautionary tale.

Instead, he found himself deposited into the surreal quiet of a Thai train car, his memory a torn map and his soul still somewhere mid-air. Bangkok to Sisaket—ten hours of purgatory on rails, an inexplicable sense of calm washing over him like warm rain, asking nothing in return. Peace— artificial, maybe, but peace nonetheless.

He was now in a land he didn't know, among people he didn't recognize, unable to communicate and unsure he even wanted to. He was married, apparently. Tattooed, inexplicably. Fragmented. Humbled. And yet... somehow at home. Like the universe had grown impatient with his wandering and finally yanked him into stillness, said: Enough.

Was it fate? Karma? Dumb luck? Or was it the culmination of every choice, every woman, every sidestep and misstep, finally cashing in their receipts? Hard to say. Willie didn't have the language for it yet. But he did know this much: someone—or more likely, someones—had moved heaven and earth to get him here. Risked. Acted. Believed.

For that, he felt gratitude. Or something adjacent to it. But the questions—too many, too jagged—kept him from fully stepping into it. Not yet. First, he needed clarity.

The first question?

He rolled up his sleeve, blinked at the unfamiliar ink burned into his skin, and squinted into the morning sun like it might offer a translation...

When did I get this tattoo... and what the hell does it say?

Scene 9

Chitra, Thailand &
What The Phram!

Willie hadn't had time to make sense of much—his memory of the last four days was little more than a flickering slideshow: city lights bending sideways, train wheels hammering out Morse code in the distance, Tuk's silence bouncing around the cab of that beat-up truck like a ghost that forgot what it came to say. He wasn't sure if he'd slept or blacked out or just drifted like a balloon someone let go of. But there was no mistaking it now: he was far, far from anything resembling a handhold. No phone. No map. No definitive recall of how he'd gotten from Tokyo's back alleys to a dirt road somewhere outside

Sisaket—or more importantly why—with a stranger driving him deeper into the fold like it was the most natural thing in the world.

And yet, the last thing he expected—the absolute last thing—was to step out of that truck and fall straight into the eyes of Wasum. Let alone Chitra.

Wasum was supposed to be back on the porch minding the whiskey for his transformed return and he hadn't allowed himself to even think about Chitra for months. She was the ghost of a different kind of possibility, the road not taken because he couldn't afford another detour. Beautiful, magnetic, maybe even meant-for-him in some karmic ledger—but he'd let that thread go cold on purpose. He had to.

And yet here they were.

Willie didn't see it coming. Didn't even have time to brace. It was like catching a left cross from a boxer you didn't know was in the ring.

One second he was blinking against the sun, trying to figure out where the hell he'd landed—and the next, he was flat on his back against a bundle of rice stalks, looking up at two faces that belonged to entirely different clouds of thought. Faces that shouldn't have been here. Faces that said everything and nothing all at once.

He tried to speak. Nothing came. His throat felt like he'd swallowed sand. His body was still in some kind of jetlagged, whiskey-laced shock, but his heart knew exactly what time it was. It was reckoning time. And somehow, somehow, these women—this strange village, this buffalo, this godforsaken tattoo—were all part of it.

Wasum was the first to move. Barefoot and steady, she knelt beside him without a word. No tears, no more theatrics. Just a hand—small, warm, certain—resting on his shoulder. Chitra followed. There was grace in her presence. She didn't speak at first, just tilted her head the way someone does when they're studying a long-lost face in an old photograph. She looked at him like she'd known for months he'd end up right here. Like this field had been waiting on him the whole damn time.

Willie tried to rise but the earth still had a hold on him. Or maybe it was the weight of what he didn't know yet. He felt a pressure behind the eyes, not tears, just... strain. Like every unanswered question was trying to punch its way out of his skull.

Wasum slid her arm under his, Chitra the other, and they gave him a gentle tug. "Come on, big guy," Wasum said with that half-smirk he remembered, the one that always came before a truth you didn't want to hear but needed to. "You're safe."

That word landed heavy.

Safe.

But safe from what?

Or worse—safe for what?

Because the moment he stood—propped between two women from completely different acts in the play—he felt the question hit him like a second wind:

Had he just been rescued... or claimed?

There was no answering it yet. Not here. Not now. But the look in Chitra's eyes—part tenderness, part ancient recognition—suggested this was no accident. This wasn't kindness, or coincidence. This was choreography. And he was late to the rehearsal.

He brushed the dust from his pants, nodded like a man trying to remember the right words in a foreign country, and followed them toward the stilt house ahead.

Behind him, the sun shown through the trees, casting long shadows across the field beyond the house.

In front of him?

A mystery old as the hills and written in a language his heart understood, even if his head didn't.

Not yet.

By now, Tuk and the old man had slipped away, their quiet departure unnoticed in the emotional static. It was just the three of them now—three lives once scattered, now braided by fate and circumstance—ambling toward the house in a slow, reverent procession.

They guided Willie up the half-dozen stairs to a wide, wraparound patio that creaked like old floorboards in a cathedral. Wasum broke off without a word and disappeared through the front door. Chitra stayed close, her hand still on Willie's arm, gently steering him to a weathered chair near the far end of the veranda where the house gave way to open air and wide sky. She eased him down like a man made of glass, then settled beside him with the kind of grace that made you forget how much strength it took to hold yourself together.

Before them stretched a quiet sea of green—rice fields in regimented rows, stitched with trees and crisscrossed with veins of water and raised earthen rows. Somewhere out there, a water buffalo groaned. Somewhere inside him, something deeper shifted.

Willie could feel her eyes on him.

"What the hell happened?" he asked, still looking down, his voice low and hoarse. "Every time a memory tries to surface, it just... slips. Kyoto Station is the last thing I can see clearly. After that, it's like trying to grab smoke."

"It'll come, Win," Chitra said softly, like she'd said it before, like she'd been rehearsing it in her heart every day since he vanished. Her voice was warm. Knowing. Tired. "Some things take time."

"How much do you know?" he asked, turning to face her fully now.

A creak from the door cut the moment like a blade through silk, and Wasum reappeared, her arms loaded like a bartender at last call—pitcher of tea, two beers, a bottle of whiskey, and three mismatched glasses.

"Boilermaker?" she said, a dry grin curling at one corner of her mouth.

"Does a bear shit in the woods?" Willie snapped, the familiar bark of humor giving him a flicker of self-recognition.

She set the drinks down and took her seat without ceremony. Willie poured, drank, and leaned forward, elbows on knees.

"So what do you guys know?" he said, voice rising now, the edge of panic starting to lick at the calm. "Help me fill in some blanks here, goddamnit."

He turned toward Chitra, rolled his right arm over, and jabbed a finger at the ink just below the crook. The skin still slightly raised, the edges of the tattoo dark and deliberate.

"Let's start with this tattoo."

Without hesitation, Chitra spoke—within the first few syllables, the air seemed to still. Thoughts scattered. Joints loosened. The porch, the space, the whole earth seemed to hush like children around a campfire anticipating a ghost story.

There was something in her cadence. Not just the softness of her voice, but the certainty curled around each word. Maybe it was the quiet weight of broken English, shaped by intention and soul. Maybe it was the way she carried wisdom like jasmine carries scent—gently, invisibly, yet impossible to ignore. Or maybe it was because, in that moment, she became something more than herself. She became truth in human form. And when truth speaks, you shut up and listen.

She turned to Willie, eyes glowing deep with time.

"The tattoo, Win... it is not just a tattoo. It is ancient vision. Given to you by most respected Phram in Thailand. It is... protection, clarity, blessing. A gift, very high."

Gesturing upwards her voice floated, soft and steel all at once.

"From the moment I hear your voice, I know. You are the other half of my spirit. I was forced to marry when I was young. It is... our way, here. But even then, I know you. I dream of you. Throughout my life... you remain."

She glanced toward the field, as if retrieving something she'd buried long ago.

"I was given rare permission by the Monks to divorce when I was twenty-four. Because of you. Not you, in body— but because you were coming. For the next twenty-four years, I waited. Knowing. My grandmother—she knew you. When I was small, she told me of a vision: a farang from distant shore. My husband was coming. You."

Willie blinked. The drink in his hand suddenly felt small. Her words, impossibly vast.

"I never get angry when you say no to me before, Win. I never worried. I knew our story was already written. In this life. Or the next."

She motioned gently with her hand, circling the air.

"When Wasum say I should call you... I say no. No need. You will call. You will come. I don't push the river."

She poured him more whiskey, not as a gesture of kindness, but as ritual.

"When you call Wasum from Japan, and she call my brother Dacha, we know. We all know. There is only one place for you to come: home."

She leaned closer now. Her voice dipped low. Sacred. "But you were not going to make it on your own."

"The Phram—the holy man—he was told it was time now by my father, also a well-respected Sage in Thailand. The same man you met, with Tuk... my son. This Phram live in our village, Win. His family do the Sak Yant for many generations. Hong Kong people, Taiwan people, they travel to see him. Japan people come. He only choose a few."

Willie said nothing. Couldn't. Just sat there, the sting of rice field dust and incense in his nose, the weight of destiny pressing against his ribs.

"Dacha arranged a flight for him to Tokyo. For you. To protect you. This would happen anyway one day—but now, it was urgent. He do meditation. Prayers. Chanting. And spirit tell him what to give."

She paused here, hand to her own back.

"He is same Phram who give me the red boat. On my back. It means you will return. For you... he give words. This is... very rare. Tattoo is always symbols. Always. Never words. He tell Dacha...before he prepare ink and the bamboo stick and needle to start the ceremony, he never see words before in vision. Only his father see before, once, many years ago."

She nodded solemnly.

"To write words on skin in Thailand... it mean you invite gods to special part of your spirit. They may bless. They may tear down you. But it open a gate."

Willie's hands trembled just a little. He looked down at the dark etching on his arm. What had once seemed like a mistake now pulsed with ancestral gravity.

"Win," she said, placing a hand on his knee, "the tattoo say, ซัมไล้ ลืออนซาน นิรันดร์... Chitra Lyonsan Eternal."

There was no reaction at first. Just a silence that rang out like a bell. Then slowly, deliberately, Willie turned his head—not away, but through her. Past her. Then toward Wasum, who sat quietly, listening, a tear slipping down her cheek like a prayer.

She smiled, nodded.

A simple, affirming nod.

Willie blinked. Took a sip. Set the glass down like it had grown heavy.

And in that moment, the whole mad pilgrimage—the long flight, the drink, the alley, the blur, the train, the rice, the tattoo—all of it shrank into a pinpoint. Into nothing. It wasn't about any of it anymore. It wasn't about the collapse.

It was about the crossing. Chitra recognized his understanding.

In this moment he found himself on the sacred side of the great torii—the hidden gate only fools and prophets ever see. And on the other side, he was no longer Willie Lyonsan, the broken American, the grieving son, the vanished man.

He was *claimed.*

Not by Chitra. Not even by himself.

But by the story...

And not just any story—his. One that had been inked onto the bones of time itself, long before he ever stumbled into the illusion of authorship.

Behind the veil of everything he thought he'd known, he was beginning to see it:

His path hadn't been found.

It had been *remembered.*

After a long stretch of introspective silence, like thick air that lingers behind unspoken truths, Wasum finally cleared her throat.

"That ring," she said softly, pointing at his finger. "And the marriage license... the one in that envelope you've been carrying around like a map back to reality... My cousin prepared it in Bangkok. Overnighted it to Dacha in Tokyo."

Willie looked down, twisting the ring idly with his thumb, the cool metal suddenly feeling heavier.

"Getting you out of Japan through Haneda was risky," she continued. "We wanted documents that would carry some weight if they ran into trouble at the airport. There are some official medical transport documents in there too. All manufactured. Forged, but... convincing."

A pause, not for drama but honesty.

"They're not real, Willie. You're not actually married." A breath. "Not in a legal sense, anyway."

Willie was quiet.

He didn't say Oh thank God, or laugh in relief. He didn't pull off the ring and toss it on the table. He just sat there, eyes dimmed with the weight of everything that had happened—and everything that hadn't. And maybe that was the saddest part.

After all he'd just heard from Chitra—of spirits and visions, of names known before they were ever spoken—and with memories of the inexplicable dialing of her phone at the vortex all those months ago in Cave Creek now flooding back into focus, the legal non-bindingness of it all felt... less than nothing. If anything, it was disappointing. Maybe even heartbreaking.

Not because he'd fallen in love with her in the last twenty minutes. Not because some romantic flame had rekindled. But because something ancient and ineffable had just wrapped its arms around him.

Chitra leaned in, and though she didn't touch him, it felt like she did. "Not by paper," she said gently. "But maybe by something more old."

Willie nodded, slowly. "Yeah," he said, voice low. "That's the part I believe."

From there, they didn't speak for a while. Wasum eventually rose and walked into the house, leaving the two of them alone on the porch. The breeze had shifted. The day was cooling.

Chitra refilled her tea and sat back down beside him. The mood between them didn't shimmer or flirt. It grounded. Anchored. They weren't two people caught up in the flush of fate. They were two halves of something that'd been adrift now coming to rest in the same place again. Not arranged by family. Arranged by the gods. And not for a ceremony. For a path.

"I always knew you would come," she said softly, almost to herself. "Not because I wait. Because I remember."

Willie didn't quite understand the words. But he didn't need to. Something inside him heard them anyway.

They sat in silence again. It wasn't heavy. It was sacred.

And when the sun finally dipped below the tree line and shadows stretched long across the fields, Willie felt, for the first time, maybe since he was cast to solve the riddle as a child in Beaverton, that he hadn't just been pulled out of one life. He'd been walked into another.

Wasum poked her head out the door, "Let me show you where you're sleeping, Willie. You must be damn tired."

They stood—Chitra with an ease that seemed bred from the soil itself, Willie a little slower, like a man walking in borrowed bones. As they made their way to the door, Chitra motioned for him to go ahead, he did, but after a couple steps he stopped and turned, facing her.

He placed a hand—gentle but deliberate—on each of her shoulders. "Thank you," he said, his voice stripped of armor, of wit, of anything but truth. A raw little offering.

Chitra looked downwards. Before she could respond he'd turned and continued his quiet march toward the doorway.

"You're in here," Wasum said, motioning toward what looked like an insulated box off to the side of a large great room, its white paneling a stark contrast to the weathered teak and woven bamboo of the rest of the house.

"You're putting me in the freezer," Willie said with a half-grin, the first in days.

"Yes, that is exactly what I'm doing," Wasum said, matching his grin. "Need to cool your ass off."

Willie stopped short of stepping inside. He faced Wasum, the grin gone. "Thank you," he said. Same eyes. Same tone. Like gratitude had suddenly become his native tongue.

She gave him a pat on the back—not just friendly, but familial. "Sleep well, Willie."

And he did. Not because the bed was comfortable (it wasn't), or because the room was quiet (crickets and frogs ran an all-night symphony just outside the walls), but because for the first time in too long, Willie felt... placed. Like some small part of him had been claimed by the earth again.

The couple of weeks that followed blurred at the edges, not because they were forgettable, but because they were sacred. And sacred things, I've found, are often remembered not in order but in feeling.

Chitra took him riding on her motorbike—a little silver Honda that coughed when it started and purred once it warmed up. She wore a baseball hat, backwards, glancing back every now and then just to make sure he was still holding on—not to her, but to the idea that this strange new life might not be a mistake.

They rode out past the village boundaries, past fields where water buffalo stood ankle-deep in muddy water like retired sentries. They stopped at makeshift, roadside food restaurants with rusty tin roofs and women who cooked with hands that didn't measure, only knew. He ate everything they gave him—no questions, no hesitation. Chitra teased him with mock suspicion, "Where you from, Win? Why you like Thai food so much?" And he'd just smile and keep chewing.

He never once got sick. Not even a whisper of stomach rebellion. She noticed. It meant something to her.

Temples marked every path like sentinels of stillness. Some were modest and worn, others were so ornate they looked like they'd been pulled from a dream and planted in the dirt. Two, sometimes three in a day. Monks would nod solemnly, their eyes soft, as if they recognized something in Willie he hadn't quite recognized in himself yet.

One monk, older than all the others, held Willie's wrist and rubbed the underside with his thumb before tying a white thread around it. The gesture was small. Sacred.

Final. Willie didn't ask what it meant. He just nodded, and let the moment be what it was.

Everywhere they went, someone knew Chitra. Or they knew her family. Or they knew of the quiet American who had somehow—without trying—earned their blessing. Smiles came easily. No one asked too much.

Chitra never rushed. She never explained more than necessary. She let Willie rediscover his body in silence. Let the sunlight and chili peppers and miles of open road do their work.

They didn't talk about Tokyo. Not yet. Not about what happened. Not about what it meant. They were still circling it. Like two people orbiting a fire neither one of them was ready to step into.

But something had shifted.

You could feel it in the pauses between words. In the way she let her hand linger just a little longer when helping him off the bike. In the way he looked at her when she wasn't watching.

Whatever this was—they were starting to remember it. Or maybe they were reinventing it. Either way, it was beginning again.

They drifted farther than usual one day—past the rice paddies, past the familiar villages, past even the range of

Chitra's easy confidence. South, toward the Cambodian border. The road got quieter. The landscape changed—denser, older somehow. More trees. Fewer people. As if the world had bowed slightly in reverence to whatever lay ahead.

The temple they found wasn't one Chitra recognized. It emerged slowly, as they rounded a bend in the road—part jungle, part myth. Portions of it looked as though it had grown up from the dirt like trees. Stone worn smooth by time and footsteps. Other parts were clearly new—clean edges, fresh paint, the unmistakable scent of recent construction. Progress standing beside history like a younger sibling eager to be taken seriously.

They walked without speaking, letting their feet and whatever spirit lived there guide them. At one point they passed into the shadow of a tall, newly built structure—something grand and clearly sacred, though neither of them had context for what, exactly, they were seeing. The door to the building was massive, carved from wood so rich and dark it looked almost wet. Dragons coiled in the design, their eyes set with flecks of green stone. The place vibrated. Not loudly, but unmistakably.

As they lingered a short distance from the entrance, a monk from inside caught sight of them through a narrow window and paused. Two other monks were passing by just then—with long stares that didn't invite questions. Chitra stiffened.

"We shouldn't be here," she said quietly, already turning to go.

But the monk from inside opened the door and stepped out, barefoot and calm. His face was lined like a Master. His eyes found Willie immediately. He said something in Thai—gentle, measured.

Chitra responded briefly, bowing her head.

Then she turned to Willie. "He's invited us inside," she said, almost whispering. "He say... he see something in your eye. From the window."

Willie blinked, unsure what to make of that.

They removed their shoes.

The staircase leading up to the door was wide, white marble veined with gold. On each side, two enormous naga—serpent-dragons carved in impossible detail—twisted up the balustrades, their scales catching the light like coins under water. Off to the right, a giant Buddha—calm, massive, and unmoving—watched them climb.

At the top, the monk opened one of the ornate doors. It groaned like a ship hull. Inside was a hall so grand it stopped them both.

The floors were rich red carpet. Chandeliers hung like frozen fireworks from a high ceiling. And at the far end—set high on a pedestal that almost glowed in the filtered light—stood a golden Buddha that had to be twenty feet tall. Maybe more. Not gaudy. Not boastful. Just... undeniable.

They stayed quietly in the back and sat on the floor. The monk stood with them.

It was still. Prayers murmured up front. Every so often, one of the monks would glance back toward them with a look that wasn't angry, but puzzled. Like a line had been crossed in the sand, and yet... no one stopped them.

After a time, the monk motioned for them to stand. Willie and Chitra rose.

The monk approached Willie and spoke softly, rhythmically, as if reciting something not entirely his own. A few dozen words. Eyes never leaving Willie's. Then he smiled.

Willie, unsure what else to do, returned the smile.

Chitra bowed—deep and reverent, her hands pressed together in prayer at her forehead. Willie followed suit, though his version looked more like a man clumsily mimicking a dance he didn't know the steps to. Still, it was earnest.

The monk smiled again. No mockery in it. Just kindness.

Then they walked out.

At the base of the stairs, they slipped their shoes back on in silence.

Chitra broke it. "You have magic power, Win," she said, not looking at him. "This never happens. Monk explained me—this is the new Ubosot. Sacred building. Center of the wat. Only monks allowed inside. Never regular people. Never farang. Never. This monk saw you from window. Saw something. He say... he saw vision. That he must bring you inside. He pray for you, Win."

Willie said nothing.

He couldn't.

They walked slowly around the rest of the wat in silence, each step softer than the last. Not out of fear. But because something had been named inside that room— something he didn't yet have words for. And maybe never would.

But it was real.

As they approached the motorbike to head back, he could feel it in his chest, like a bell rung quietly in a deep cave.

Not much of a passenger by nature, Chitra had started letting Willie drive the motorbike. It wasn't a declaration, just something that happened one morning without ceremony. She handed him the keys like she was passing him a brush and a canvas he didn't know he owned.

Things were shifting inside Willie—subtle, tectonic shifts. Nothing loud, just a quiet rearranging of truths.

The ride back to the farm that day was... dreamlike. That was the word he landed on later, though it didn't quite do it justice. There was a kind of bone-deep freedom that buzzed through him as they drifted along those remote backroads—narrow ribbons of dirt and cracked asphalt threading their way through open fields, sleepy villages, and a horizon that always seemed to lean toward dusk.

Bliss. That's what he called it. Not the cheap kind. Not the manic euphoria of a man escaping his past. This was different. This was arrival. A kind of quiet joy that lives at the cellular level.

Somehow, with almost no instruction, Willie navigated across a foreign countryside like he'd been born to it. He wasn't thinking. He wasn't planning. He was moving— through a place that should've felt alien but instead felt eerily familiar. Like muscle memory. Like maybe, just maybe, he wasn't lost out here. Maybe he was remembering.

When they finally rolled into the farm, the sun was leaning low and everything had gone gold. Chitra's phone buzzed as they parked. She answered it, speaking Thai in the soft, half-laughing tone she used when it was family. It was Wasum. She had gone to Bangkok to be with her Mom and sister several days before.

Willie dismounted, stretched his back, and stared out across the fields—their endless rhythm, the soundless sermon they gave to anyone who would just sit still long enough to listen.

In the middle of Chitra's string of Thai he heard "Oscar."

He turned fast.

Chitra smiled and handed him the phone.

"Hey, Willie!" She said, "You have a visitor coming the day after tomorrow..."

He blinked, the gears turning. "Oscar!" he beamed.

"Yep!" She said. "He gets in around midnight, gonna crash in Bangkok, then hop the train to Sisaket the next night."

There was a beat of silence.

And then, Willie grinned. Big. Lopsided. Like a man who'd just found an old song buried in a dusty box.

"Well, I'll be damned," he said. "This'll be something else."

And he wasn't wrong.

It would be.

Scene 10

Oscar Visits

The night before I was to arrive Chitra informed Willie she'd arranged for him to use Tuk's truck to drive into Sisaket. She handed Willie the keys. No fanfare, no explanation beyond the practical.

"You'll be more comfortable in the truck," she told him, matter-of-fact. "Take your time. All the time you want. This is an important visit."

And maybe it was the way she said it—this is an important visit—like she wasn't talking about me, not exactly. Like maybe she was talking about what Willie might remember in the space between now and when he had to drive back to the farm.

The train was due in at six sharp, which meant Willie needed to leave around four. By 3:45, Chitra was already tapping gently on his door, her voice barely more than breath.

"Wake up, Win... you don't want to be late."

She had a tumbler of coffee ready—black and strong, no sugar. She pressed two folded notes of 1,000 baht each into his palm and smiled. "Don't worry about anything," she said. "This is an important day."

He pulled her into a quiet hug—a language they'd begun speaking more fluently without words—and stepped out into the waiting dark.

The drive into Sisaket was mostly empty road and the company of early stars. That liminal hour between night and dawn has a strange sort of magic to it. The world feels paused, like even the future is still asleep.

Willie arrived fifteen minutes ahead of schedule and parked the truck just off the station. He stepped out and breathed in the quiet, familiar shape of morning: the horizon beginning to yawn in a golden stretch, the low tin-roof shacks across the tracks just starting to stir. A few lights flickered on. A dog barked once, then thought better of it.

The train station was still, save for the rhythmic squeak of a ceiling fan trying not to fall apart. And in that moment, standing there on the platform, Willie was hit by a strange déjà vu—a ripple of memory from the morning he first arrived. The stillness. The air. The waiting. Like the world was handing him the same moment twice, just to see what he'd do with it this time.

Now, Thailand doesn't share America's hang-ups about alcohol and the hour of day. Nobody bats an eye if you have a beer with your rice and eggs at 6 a.m. It's not indulgence—it's just living.

And so, informed by local custom (and a deep understanding of who he is at his core), Willie scanned the market area across the tracks for a place that looked like it might serve something cold and fermented with breakfast. He spotted a man with a hose, washing down the stoop in front of a narrow shop, and the glow of a TV behind the window. Good sign.

Willie made a mental note to check it out after the train arrived.

And then, in the distance—a low hum. The train.

He felt it before he heard it. Like thunder miles off. Familiar, but not yet visible. It had been a long stretch since he'd seen me, and whatever we'd both been carrying around —grief, confusion, the weight of too many unanswered questions—it all softened a little in that moment.

Willie stood at the edge of the platform, hands in his pockets, eyes scanning the tracks, a quiet heat rising in his chest. Gratitude, maybe. Or just the strange joy of knowing that, for the next stretch of hours, he'd have someone beside him who knew his whole damn story and never asked for a rewrite.

And that?

That mattered more than he could explain.

The train hissed in like an iron ghost, slow and inevitable, dragging the early light behind it. Willie took a step closer to the edge of the platform, heart beating somewhere between anticipation and disbelief. It wasn't just that I was arriving—it was who was arriving. Someone who remembered him before the unraveling. Someone who could still see the man beneath the layers.

The train hissed to a stop. Doors opened. A small crowd dispersed across the platform, most of them locals returning from a city run, sleepy-eyed and loaded with plastic bags of goods they couldn't find in the village.

And then he saw me—standing there in the open doorway of the third car, squinting into the rising sun, one hand on the strap of a beat-up duffel, the other hanging loose by my side like I'd just stepped off stage from a long-forgotten play.

Willie didn't wave.

Neither did I.

We just looked at each other.

Two men, both changed, both still the same.

It was Willie who stepped forward first. I followed.

By the time we met halfway across the platform, neither of us had spoken a word. Willie reached out, pulled me in, and for the first time in a very long time, I felt that rare kind of embrace between old friends who've walked through separate fires and come out still carrying the matchbooks.

I won't lie. My throat tightened. His eyes glistened.

"Jesus, Willie," I finally said. "You look like the land grew you from scratch."

He grinned, lopsided and soft. "Feels that way."

And it did. There was something in his eyes—clear, grounded, wide open. Not polished. Not enlightened. Just... planted. I swear, it was like he'd been standing on this soil since birth and only just now found his way back to it.

"I don't know what you've been drinking," I said, hoisting my bag over my shoulder, "But whatever it is, bottle it. You're glowing like a damn Bodhisattva."

"Come on," he said, brushing a sleeve across his cheek. "Let's grab a beer before we start talking nonsense."

We crossed the tracks and headed toward the cafe he'd spotted—barely open, fan spinning overhead, a TV playing a Thai soap opera no one would watch. The owner, still barefoot from washing down the steps, looked up and nodded. No words. Just recognition. Two men at sunrise, thirsty and curious.

We settled into plastic chairs at a metal table out front. He ordered a couple Leos and, after a moment of pause, two shots of Thai whiskey. The woman behind the counter brought them without question.

The beers sweated in the outside air. The whiskey glowed amber in the tiny glasses.

We clinked them together without ceremony.

"To whatever the hell this is," I said.

"To making sense of it," he replied.

And we drank.

In that moment I couldn't help but think: the two of us here—connected deeper than blood, stitched together by nearly five decades of scraped knees, broken hearts, half-baked dreams and moments of grace that never made the highlight reel. I've watched Willie's life twist and tangle in ways that would get a movie script laughed out of the pitch room—absurd, beautiful, tragic, and somehow always with a grin at the edge of the wreckage. And now here we were,

9,000 miles from everything we once called normal, sitting under a rusted tin roof at six in the goddamn morning, in a forgotten corner of Thailand, nursing boilermakers like it was the most natural thing in the world. Just the two of us and a day old soap opera flickering behind the counter. Only Willie. I swear to God—only Willie.

The whiskey bit like it always does, but the beer followed easy, and for a few long, quiet minutes, we just sat there. Watching the sun rise through the haze. Listening to a shopkeeper sweep her stoop. Smelling the charcoal from nearby street stalls coming to life.

Eventually, I leaned back, stared at him, really stared. "Alright, Willie. I've been patient. But what in God's name happened out here? The last I heard, you were meditating your way through Japan and now—now you're barefoot in rural Thailand, with a wife, a stepson, a buffalo, and a tattoo that looks like it was inked by the Buddha himself."

Willie grinned, took another pull from his beer, and looked out across the market like the answer might drift in on the steam from a pot of rice.

"It's a hell of a story," he said.

And the way he said it. I could tell—it wasn't just his story anymore.

"Oscar, my friend," he said, steady now, voice soft but tuned with intention, "I could tell you the details of Japan and it would sound like I was making it up—and you *know* the outlandish shit I've rolled myself into, and out of. Wasum's probably given you the broad strokes already, and I'll fill in the colors when the time's right. But what I want to share with you now, Brother, goes to the marrow. And you... you will hear it like no one else could."

He paused, looked out across the waking market, then back at me. And right then, I saw it again—that glow in his face, not performative or forced, but *placed*. Like someone had finally set him in the exact groove he was carved to rest in.

"You've been with me through it all," he continued. "You know the haunting displacement I've carried around in my bones since we were kids. That constant itch just under the skin. Like I'd missed a turn somewhere early on and was damned to wander forever looking for it. And I *tried*, man. I really did. All the places, all the people, all the beautiful wreckage I left in my wake—and, Cave Creek, the desert nights, the fire pits and the friendships, that whole world I truly forged into family... I was convinced that was it. My place. My people. My peace. And it is... but..."

He leaned back, exhaled through his nose like he was finally letting something loose that had been rattling around inside for too long.

"But even there, Oscar—in the middle of all that good —I'd lay in bed at night with that same weight on my chest. That low, dull hum of *nope*. Like I was playing the right song in the wrong key. Like I was close, but not quite... *home*."

I didn't say a word. Didn't need to. Just kept my eyes on him and let him go.

"And then this happened," he said, motioning vaguely around us, to the sunrise, the smells, the hum of early motorbikes and birdsong. "Thailand. This strange and holy turn I didn't plan, couldn't have predicted, and sure as hell didn't understand. I woke up in it—literally—and for a while I thought it was another version of the chaos I always seem to attract. But it's not."

His voice dropped an octave, his eyes shining—not with sentiment, but truth.

"I'm not *trying* to belong here, Oscar. I *do*. From the second my feet hit this soil, I felt it. In the land. In the air. In the eyes of people I didn't know who seemed to already know me. And especially... *especially* in Chitra."

He said her name not like a man naming a lover, but like a monk naming a truth. Sacred. Grounded.

"I keep trying to frame it in something familiar, and I can't. I don't *want* to love her. I'm not deciding it. It's just... *there.* Like a tether from another life. Something older than time. I look at her and it's like recognizing your own handwriting in a letter you forgot you wrote."

He pulled up his sleeve and pointed at the tattoo.

"Even this," he said, brushing his fingers lightly across the ink, "This isn't decoration. It's not a souvenir. It was *given* to me. And not by accident. The ritual, the prayers, the monk—Oscar, this wasn't ink. This was a key. It unlocked something. Even in the absence of any awareness it was even being given to me, I felt it. Like the world nudged a piece of me into place that had been floating just out of reach my whole life."

I looked at it—the intricate lines, the faded swelling, the faint shimmer of oil still soaked into the skin. And I believed him. With every damn cell in my body.

He looked back out at the market, blinking against the light now creeping across the café floor.

"For the first time—maybe ever—I don't want to go. I don't need to look around the next bend for the answer. Because the ache is gone. That restless, ceaseless ache that's followed me from birth... it's just *gone.* I feel like I've come back to somewhere I was meant to be all along, but forgot how to find. And Chitra... she's not the destination. She's the compass. She was *always* pointing me here, even before we met."

He shook his head, smiling, but there was a crack in the voice, a weight.

"I don't know how to explain this to anyone else. Hell, I barely understand it myself. But you... *you*, Oscar... you're the only one who's known me long enough, deep enough, to understand what it means when I say: I'm home."

And with that, the silence came—not awkward, not waiting, just present. Thick with truth.

I looked at him—my brother in everything but name—and saw a man who'd finally laid down a burden I didn't even know he still carried.

And in that moment, I didn't want to dissect it. I didn't want to offer analysis or metaphors or even a reply.

I just raised my glass, and he raised his, and we drank again.

Because sometimes, the holy thing to do when someone finds their center...is to sit in the sun beside them, and let it rise.

The silence remained, thick as temple smoke. The kind only two people who've lived *deeply* through the same fires can share without needing to speak.

I looked at him and nodded—not because I understood everything, but because I believed it. Believed *him*. And in return, he nodded back. That old look we'd exchanged a thousand times before any of this—through hangovers, heartbreaks, court dates, miracles, all of it. A simple truth passed between us: *I see you. Still. Always.*

And then the moment faded. Not lost—just placed on a shelf where it could glow quietly.

"C'mon," Willie said, pushing his chair back. "Let's show you what home looks like."

The days that followed moved like honey in the heat— slow, golden, and impossible to separate into clean edges. I couldn't tell you what happened first or last, just that it all belonged together.

We spent hours on the road, me riding shotgun in Tuk's dusty old truck or clinging to the back of Willie's motorbike, both of us laughing like kids dodging time. The sun chased us down red dirt lanes, the horizon wide and forgiving. Locals nodded as we passed, not with curiosity, but with something closer to recognition—like they'd known Willie for years and I was just a familiar extension of whatever he'd become.

There were roadside stands where the smell of garlic and oil floated heavy in the air, and Willie would point at a dish with that confident half-smile like he'd grown up eating it. We'd sit in plastic chairs too small for grown men, drink cold beer straight from the bottle, and let the sweat run down our faces while the old woman behind the grill moved with the grace of a symphony conductor.

Sometimes Chitra would join us—quiet at first, but sharp-eyed and amused at our antics. She had a laugh like wind chimes—unexpected and bright—and when she let it out, it made the moment feel like it had been waiting just for that sound. She didn't try to keep up with us; she didn't need to. She belonged in every scene without ever having to announce herself.

One evening, we wandered out to a temple set back in the trees. The kind of place that seems to pulse with its own heartbeat. The monks said little, but watched us closely. One of them—old and deeply still—took Willie's wrist and tied a thread of white around it, murmuring something I didn't understand but felt. Willie didn't flinch. He just bowed, deeply, and when he stood, I swear something invisible had been added to him. Or maybe just uncovered. Chitra motioned for me to kneel and receive the sacred strings of acceptance too. The moment... It moved me deeply.

There were long meals by lantern light, fireflies drifting in and out like lazy sparks. The three of us at a long wooden table, talking about everything and nothing. One night we'd drink too much and laugh too loud, and another night we'd just sit in the hush of the farm, the air thick with night sounds, saying nothing at all. I watched Willie move through it all with a kind of grace I'd never seen in him before—like a man who finally stopped asking if he belonged and started living like he *knew.*

And somehow, it felt like I was seeing him again for the first time. Not reinvented. Just... *realized.*

When it came time to go, we didn't rush. I packed up quietly, loaded my bag into the truck, and drove back to the train station in Sisaket just as the sun was beginning to flirt with the idea of setting. The sky had that golden-pink hue it gets when the day is already turning into a story.

We didn't talk much on the drive. We didn't have to.

At the station we stood on the platform, just like a few mornings before—but everything was different now.

The train was due any minute. I had my bag slung low across my back, the same one I'd arrived with, but heavier now. Not with things, but with *knowing.*

"I can't explain it," I said, looking off toward the horizon. "But I get it. I get all of it. You don't need to convince me of anything, Brother."

Willie nodded, chewing the inside of his cheek.

"You're not lost, you're *found*." And I didn't mean it in a loud, born-again way. Not in a Facebook-quote-on-a-sunset way. In the real way. The *earned* way. "And seeing it on you... hell, man, it makes me believe maybe I'll get found too."

Willie stepped forward, pulled me in for a long hug—the kind where you say everything you can't say in words.

"You will," He said into my shoulder. "And if not, you know where I'll be."

The train's whistle blew once—low and lonely.

I pulled away and looked him square in the eye.

"We're good?"

"Better than ever," Willie said. "We're *right*."

A pause.

And with a smile, I said "See you soon", turned and boarded.

Willie stayed right there on the platform, hands in his pockets, as the train groaned into motion. He didn't wave. Just watched, steady, as the man who knew every scar and story slowly disappeared into the evening haze.

And when the last car passed and the rails went quiet, he stood for a moment longer.

Then he turned, walked back towards the truck, got in and headed...home.

Scene 11

Revelation. Redemption. Return.

By the time the train had made its first turn towards Bangkok, Willie had already started making his way back to the farm.

Seeing him standing on that platform as the train pulled away, hands in his pockets, looking like the final frame of a film no one else had the guts to make I felt good. I knew now. It all hummed just right.

And I know this, too:

He didn't go home that day.

He was already home.

Because by god, Willie Lyonsan—restless seeker, hell on wheels, walking contradiction—was no longer at a crossroads. No longer asking which way to go, no longer chasing the phantom of something better. He was found. Rooted. Planted in a soil that remembered him before he remembered himself.

And the truth is, freedom like that doesn't come easy. Not for a man like him, living the story he lived.

He'd spent a lifetime wandering. Through Midwest nights and broken-glass mornings. Through border town alleys and Tokyo blackouts. Through the arms of women who tried to love him—and the arms of women he tried to disappear inside of. Through the firestorm of Maria, and the soft, echoing memory of Lexi. Through Hui Ko's grace. Through Nina Duval's untamed passion. Through Stephanie's fearless, patient caring. Through the strange and sacred tether he shared with Louie—something beyond explanation, beyond blood.

And through it all—so much more, so many more—he kept moving. Crisscrossing open roads like a man chasing whispers. Until he landed in Cave Creek, where he built not just a life, but a soul family. The kind that holds, even across oceans. The kind that never lets go.

Through all of it.

Every misstep. Every scar. Every inexplicable miracle.

It wasn't waste.

It was altar.

And now, standing in a village most people couldn't find on a map, surrounded by people who didn't know his past but somehow still knew him, Willie finally understood: all that madness wasn't the detour. It was the design.

Because Chitra—that spirit woman with eyes like still water and a soul that hummed like a tuning fork—she didn't just arrive. She was the gravity all along. The pull he couldn't name. The silent thread through every broken moment that somehow didn't break him.

And the wildest part?

She found him after he'd been completely undone, fully unraveled—in a speck of time before his near demise. When there was nothing left but truth and bone and whatever pieces the gods chose to spare, that's when she appeared.

And he didn't even know her name.

But something deeper did.

Thailand seemed to unstop some deep, dammed river in Willie—a river that had been pressing at the walls of him for years, maybe decades. But it was Isaan specifically, that wide, rugged northeastern corner of the country, where something in the air—maybe the smoke from burning rice stalks, maybe the scent of garlic and diesel and red clay—hit his bloodstream like a chemical trigger of creative soul.

It lit him up.

I've seen Willie at the peak of his creativity—when he was wild with it, obsessed with building meaning out of chaos. But this... this was different. This was a few floors above peak. This wasn't a sprint. It was a flood.

He started writing again. Not casually. Obsessively. Said he dumped out fifty thousand words in the two months after I left—just poured it onto the pages like it had been living in him all along, waiting for him to stop fighting gravity.

And the camera—his vision behind the lens was fully resurrected.

He fell back into photography like a man falling back into himself. Not to impress. Not to sell. Not even to share. Just because he had to.

He was out every morning even before the monks started their alms walk, meandering the village roads with that same quiet intensity I'd seen years ago when he and Stephanie were chasing cowboys through dust storms for Frank Rizzo's book. That version of Willie—the one with calloused hands, tired eyes, and a lens between him and the rest of the world—that version was back. Only this time, it wasn't about the project. It wasn't about the work. It was about the seeing.

He shot temples wreathed in fog. Weathered farmers whose skin told longer stories than their words ever could. Little kids with bare feet and fierce stares. Market stalls. Motorbikes. Monks and mango carts. His portraits weren't just good—they were haunting. Like he'd finally tapped into that rare alchemy where talent meets truth.

There was vision now. Whole and matured. As if the noise in his head had finally cleared, and the lens could breathe.

"I've got something to say again," he told me in one of his messages. "And I finally stopped asking who I need to say it to."

He called me one night in the throes of a writing session. Usually we'd talk for just a few minutes, but this night, he had some things on his heart. Seems like we talked for an hour. I swear I could hear him beam through the phone. He was recalling events and obscure stories that even I struggled to remember. Bones that had long since been buried.

And then he shifted gears, and got a little introspective. The conversation carried forward a ways.

"You know," he said, voice low, "I've been thinking about them all lately."

I didn't need to ask who.

"Maria," he started, name falling like a note from a forgotten piano. "She hollowed me out. God, she wrecked me in a way I didn't think I could come back from. But you know what? She also cracked me open. She made space. She carved out a place I didn't know I'd need for Chitra."

He took a breath.

"And Lexi... hell. That girl could've set the ocean on fire if she wanted to. Those eight days...you know what, fuck it, I loved her with my fists clenched and my jaw tight. She showed me what it meant to want something so badly—no matter how wrong—you lose yourself in the chase. I'll always carry that one."

A long pause.

"Hui Ko," he said, a smile in his voice. "That was lightning. And weird. Gone too fast, never meant to stay, but she showed me that the world was bigger than I thought. That love didn't have to speak the same language to be real."

His voice lowered slightly.

"And Nina—Nina Duval! My god, what a mirror she held up in a lot of ways. Thank God she's in it." We laughed. "No kidding! She showed me things I didn't want to see. And in doing that, she gave me the choice to change a few things in myself. She didn't stick around for the change, of course— but she didn't need to."

"Stephanie?" I offered.

Willie laughed. "Stephanie was a detour I never saw coming and wouldn't change for the world. Two polar universes colliding like asteroids. She did lend comfort and a soft landing after Nina, though. What an adventure. You know, I've never did see that book. Forgot about it. Hope ol' Frank got what he wanted."

"If he didn't you'll find out eventually, even 9,000 miles away." We laughed.

"And Lou?" I asked, knowing the weight behind the name.

Willie paused. I could hear him swallow.

"Lou was the brother I didn't choose—but would've. He kept me standing more times than I can count. We lit a thousand fires and burned through even more one-sided stories. He didn't see the world the way I did, at least I don't think he did—but he saw me. Lou knew how to carry my load even when I didn't. One of a kind. I miss him every single day."

A silence stretched.

"You spent more years in Arizona than anywhere after you left Beaverton..." and before I could continue he said,

"Arizona was the dress rehearsal. It was love and loss and a hell of a lot of almosts. It was red rock and cigarette nights and learning how to break and build at the same time. That desert carved me just like the river carved those canyons. I thought it was the end of the road, in more ways than one. But, in truth, it turned out to be the edge of the map."

"All of them—all of it and every one of em'—was a verse in the song that led me here. I don't carry bitterness or regret. Not a drop. I carry gratitude. I carry honor. Because it was all pieces of the puzzle. And without them..."

He paused. I could faintly hear Chitra's soft laughter echoing in a conversation in the distance. I could tell he was listening to it too.

"...I might've missed the one piece that made the whole thing make sense."

We were sharing a dram of George Dickel 9,000 miles apart.

He said, "Let's raise a glass my friend. To the ghosts. To the ones who broke us open so we could finally let the truth in."

I raised mine, too.

We drank.

And I swear—just for a second—the wind shifted in that moment, like it was carrying names we hadn't spoken aloud in years.

He said, "You feel that, Oscar?"

Astounded, I responded, "Yes I did, Willie."

"Now that's how you honor the past and launch the soul forward. The roots and the wings", he said.

You know, he never did take that the ring off, either. Never did. Not even when he thought it was madness. Not even when he wasn't sure what it meant. Because some part of him did know.

That he wasn't married to a moment. He was married to a miracle.

It was just a few weeks after that phone call. They didn't send out invitations.

There was no save-the-date, no registry, no hashtag.

Just word-of-mouth through the village and a sunrise that burned a little brighter than usual—like even the sky knew something sacred was about to unfold.

By mid-morning, the whole damn village had gathered. Children in school uniforms, grandmothers in bright silk, monks in their saffron robes, neighbors who hadn't left their land in weeks. They came barefoot, on mopeds, by cart, some just walking hand-in-hand from across the fields.

There must've been two hundred people by the time the drums started.

Not the thundering Western kind, but soft, deliberate rhythms played on ancient hide—heartbeat music. A sound that said we are here. A sound that said the spirit is listening.

The ceremony was called Bai Sri Su Kwan, and if you've never seen it, let me tell you—it's not a wedding in the way you're used to. There's no aisle, no "here comes the bride," no exchanging of polished vows while some bored cousin records it on their phone.

No. This was different.

This was spiritual reclamation.

They called it a "calling of the kwan"—the spirit essence, the soul force, the thing in you that sometimes wanders during trauma or chaos or heartbreak. And now, finally, the community had gathered to call it all back to Willie. To anchor him. To complete him.

Willie and Chitra sat on woven mats at the center of a circle of monks and elders, wrapped in white, knees bent beneath them. A ceremonial pyramid of flowers and candles stood between them—green and gold and wild with meaning. Her father sat front and center, his posture impossibly straight, his hands folded with such grace it almost looked like prayer.

And his face. I saw the pictures.

My god, his face.

This man, who had watched his daughter carry quiet strength through the years, now beamed like the sun had chosen to rise just for her. Not a single doubt in his eyes. Not one.

Willie was barefoot, calm, eyes steady. There was no script. He didn't need one. He looked like a man who had finally remembered the words to a song he'd been humming his whole life.

The Phram placed connected strings over each of their heads to bond them together and proceeded with a very long prayer followed by sacred chanting. The elders circled them, chanting softly, rhythmically. One by one, they tied white strings around their wrists—over and over—until their arms looked like holy tapestries.

The strings weren't just symbols.

They were bindings. Of spirit to body. Of past to present. Of broken man to healed soul. By tradition, you kept them on your wrists for three days following the ceremony.

At one point, a monk held Willie's hand in both of his and whispered something that made Willie nod, eyes glassy. I don't know what was said. Doesn't matter. It landed.

Then came the final blessing.

The Phram—his voice more gravel than air now—spoke into the hush of the circle. He said Chitra's name. He said Willie's. He touched their joined heads.

And the room didn't just grow quiet.

It grew still.

Like time had paused. Like the entire universe had stopped mid-breath to say: Yes.

And when it ended, there was applause and cries of joy—full-bodied, whole-hearted joy—rice was flying everywhere.

Children danced. Men sang. Old women hugged Chitra like she'd just come back from a war. Food appeared like magic. Beer flowed. Laughter echoed.

And in the middle of it all, Willie stood next to his bride—not smiling for a camera, not playing to the crowd—but steady. Radiant. Home.

I haven't heard from Willie in a while. But I don't worry. Not like I used to. Because I know where he is. He's not drifting through cities anymore. Not losing himself in neon nights or dusty backroads or the arms of women who never asked for the whole truth. He's not chasing ghosts or dodging the quiet.

He's on the farm. He's making pictures for the ages with his trusty old fujifilm, of Isaan and of its people. He's writing.

He's with Chitra.

He's in a place where the language still escapes his mouth, but not his heart. A place where he wakes to the sound of roosters and monks and rain on a tin roof, and knows, down to the marrow, that he belongs.

He still wears the ring. Not out of obligation. Not because of law. But because something bigger than both whispered this is it, and he finally had the courage to listen.

Every story, every stumble, every godforsaken sideways turn—it all bent toward this.

Not a fairytale.

Not a finish line.

Just truth.

Real, raw, blistered truth. The kind you only find when you dig past the surface, past the distractions, past the noise— into the dirt of it. Into the soul of it. With courage and unrelenting seeking.

Willie dug that deep.

And the truth—by god—found him.

So if you're reading this, wondering if he made it, wondering if a man like him could ever find peace, let me answer it plain:

He did.

He did.

Because sometimes, the story doesn't end with answers, or even a return. It ends with arrival.

And Willie Lyonsan?

He arrived.

Right where he belongs.

Epilogue

Oscar's Final Word

Why is this story being told at all? I suppose I told you this story for the same reason anyone tells any story worth its salt—to make sense of the parts that don't. To honor a man who kept walking long after most would've laid down in the road. To understand, if only for myself, how one soul can be burned clean by the world and come out the other side somehow more—not less.

Willie Lyonsan never came back the same. And maybe that's the point.

I lost him, in a way. The version I once knew—the one who used to crash on my couch and leave half-drunk coffee mugs like paperweights on my manuscripts—he evaporated somewhere between Tokyo and Thailand. The man I found when I visited... he was quieter. Fuller. Like someone who finally made peace with a war no one else knew was raging.

And I gained something, too. Telling his story stitched something back together in me. Maybe that's selfish. Maybe that's what writing does—it tricks you into thinking you're mapping someone else's soul, only to realize you've been drawing your own heart all along.

There are mornings I still half-expect to get a call. Maybe he and Chitra will show up in Michigan one spring, tan and serene, dragging mismatched luggage and a puppy who rides a buffalo. Maybe not. Either way, I like imagining him out there. Alive. Not just breathing, but alive—in that big, unscripted, messy way that only Willie ever seemed to master.

I didn't tell you this story to wrap it up neat. I told it so you'd remember him. So you'd carry him, like I do. In that weird corner of your chest reserved for the almost sanctified, the heartbreakingly real, the strange few who stumble into our lives and leave behind something heavier than their name.

So if you ever find yourself in some sunburned corner of the world, and you hear laughter drifting from a house with too many wind chimes, and a woman humming while she boils rice—look twice.

Willie might still be out there.

As for me, I keep one thing close—an old, leather-bound journal Willie left behind, tucked in the bottom of a satchel he'd abandoned at my place years ago. The spine's cracked, pages dog-eared, corners smudged with desert dust and coffee stains. Some entries are wild and frenzied, others quiet and raw—whole pages of silence broken only by a line or two, as if the words couldn't quite catch up to the living. I don't read it often. But when I do, it feels like he's still speaking to me, low and direct, like he's leaning in across a campfire somewhere far from here. It's not a map. It's not even a record. It's a heartbeat.

And it's still going. But you'd never believe the next part...

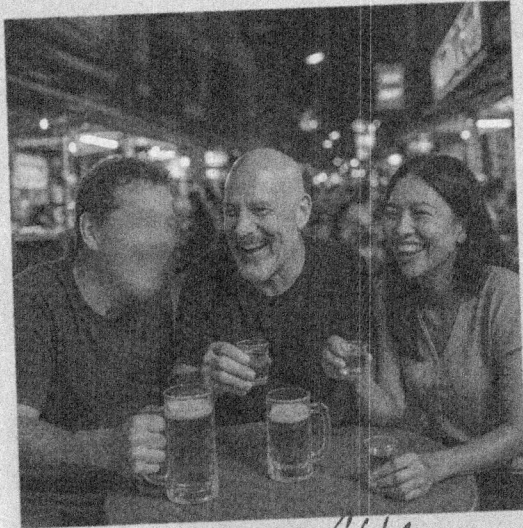

Me, Willie & Chris
Ubon 3/24

Louie

We didn't know it then, but this was the last time we were in the same place together, at the same time, without ghosts or explanations.

I remember this—it was a funny moment in Ubon Ratchathani. With Chitra's direction, I tried my hand at ordering drinks in Thai. The order was supposed to be three beers and two whiskeys—she's not a whiskey drinker.

As you can see, we got three whiskeys and two beers.

Without missing a beat, Chitra grabbed the two whiskeys and said, "Thank you, I take these," got up, and walked away. Our waitress snapped the picture at the perfect time as she sat back down.

Great memory.

And, as you can see, the legend tracks. Lou is—*as advertised.* He held that look most of the time. Wholly unimpressed.

Truly one-of-a-kind. RIP my friend.

oscarslamp.com

Selected References & Source Materials

1. Slamp, O. (1987). *Zen and the Art of Bullshit Detection*. Beaverton Press.

2. Lyonsan, W. (1999–2004). *Field Notes: Border Towns and Broken Hearts*. Unpublished manuscript.

3. Duvall, N. (2006). *You'll Never Find Me*. Self-published chapbook, 3rd printing. Now out of print.

4. Rizzo, F. (2000). *The Last Cowboys of Cochise County*. New West Publishing.

5. Lexi. (1998). *Private Letters, Mostly Burned*. Personal collection.

6. Anonymous. (n.d.). *The Jambalaya Manifesto*. Retrieved from a telephone pole in the Marigny, New Orleans.

7. Ko, H. (2011). *On Grace and Going*. NamSan House, Battle Creek, MI.

8. Slamp, O. (2024). *The Mostly True Tale of Getting Roofied in Tokyo and Waking Up Married in Rural Thailand*. Personal notes (smudged).

9. [Redacted]. (n.d.). *Untitled fragment*, retrieved from a locked drawer behind the register of a noodle shop in Sisaket. Sauce-stained.

Printed in Dunstable, United Kingdom